MW00466504

"Charlie J. Stephens hands the reader the heartbeat of the earth and the heartbeat of every living creature on it. With precise and measured prose, *A Wounded Deer Leaps Highest* is a breathtaking look into the interconnectedness of people, animals, and landscape. A pulsing novel filled with so much love and tenderness."

—MORGAN TALTY, *Night of the Living Rez*

"I wish I had this book growing up, I wish my mother had this book, and her mother, and everyone who has ever had to turn their pain into meaning. This novel feels like breathing in the lushness of the forest, where all our past memories, both difficult and joyful, greet us animals in the night."

—KALI FAJARDO-ANSTINE, *Woman of Light*

"Stephens reveals a secret and unseen world, sensitized to the dark magic of poverty and neglect in woodlands, where being othered is the cage and the key at once."

—JONATHAN T. BAILEY, *When I Was Red Clay*

"*A Wounded Deer Leaps Highest* portrays the nearly inexpressible – the blazing soul of a child who lives well outside the reach of economic, social, or familial protections. Smokey holds their flame to guide us, drawing us deeper and deeper into a bitter, forever-raining, but enfolding wilderness. Charlie J. Stephens sustains the authorial courage to stick the landing: no simplistic plot saves, no looking away."

—KARIN ANDERSON, *What Falls Away*

"In gorgeous tough prose, Charlie J. Stephens shows us childhood as a gauntlet of violences to survive—and then shows us moments of solidarity, connection, and maybe a little hope. This book broke my heart."

—ANDREA LAWLOR, *Paul Takes the Form of a Mortal Girl*

"*A Wounded Deer Leaps Highest* is a debut as wondrous as the life it portrays. In Moss River, Oregon, eight-year-old Smokey lives where no life seems possible by befriending animals, depending on Big Oak, and latching onto the moments of goodness their mother can offer. With a light touch and in beautiful prose, Charlie J. Stephens creates life and makes it matter."

—CYNTHIA NEWBERRY MARTIN, *Tidal Flats*

"*A Wounded Deer Leaps Highest* is a beautiful coming of age story dappled in a sepia glow that sparkles like Oregon rain. Charlie J. Stephens has channeled the voice of an eight-year-old child like only the most empathetic, observant, and magical writers can. Here is a novel that shows the reader how the human heart expands and grows and learns to survive in a world outside of their control."

—KEVIN SAMPSELL, Powell's Books

"I don't know when I've ever been this excited by a new voice. Smokey, the narrator of Charlie J. Stephens' *A Wounded Deer Leaps Highest*, does whatever it takes to stay alive at a time and place in which the adults can't be relied upon, and plants and animals are the most sustaining guardians. Every moment here is loving, tough, and incandescent. It's stunning."

—PAUL LISICKY, *Later: My Life at the Edge of the World*

"A subtle accounting of surviving childhood in a body and place where belonging and pain live inside of each other. Charlie J. Stephens has given us a delicate, fierce look at how young people reject the systems and violences of our parents. At the end, I wanted to start again—to know the Oregon landscape that much better, to see for just a little longer through Smokey's sensitive and lonely eyes."

—LEWIS RAVEN WALLACE, *The View from Somewhere*

"*A Wounded Deer Leaps the Highest* is a vivid and compelling novel that captures Oregon's lush and dark landscape and the sharp edges of a young person's will to survive poverty and violence. Charlie J. Stephens has carved this story into my memory with their exquisite and shocking prose."

—CHELSIA RICE, Montana Book Company

"With prose at once lyrical and precise, Smokey expertly immerses the reader in their tiny, constricted world. The people in this world are deeply wounded by toxic masculinity. Still, consolation amidst the pain and chaos can be found in a heroic, if highly unorthodox, maternal love and—above all—the companionship of animals. This is not a story that will be quickly forgotten."

—ALVIN ORLOFF, Fabulosa Books

"At times moody and violent, other times tender and curious, Charlie J. Stephens' debut novel *A Wounded Deer Leaps Highest* hits hard; it's a story about anger, self-discovery, abuse, refuge, and survival."

—TOMAS MONIZ, *All Friends Are Necessary*

"*A Wounded Deer Leaps Highest* is a beautiful and devastating glimpse into the troubled family life of eight-year old nonbinary child Smokey. Smokey and their mother's relationship is the heart of the story, and feels refreshingly honest. But be prepared! Though slim, this novel packs an emotional wallop."

—EMILY SOMBERG, Pegasus Books

A Wounded Deer Leaps Highest

A Wounded Deer
Leaps Highest

A NOVEL

Charlie J. Stephens

TORREY HOUSE PRESS

Salt Lake City • Torrey

First Torrey House Press Edition, April 2024
Copyright © 2024 by Charlie J. Stephens
All rights reserved. No part of this book may be reproduced or retransmitted in any form or by any means without the written consent of the publisher.

NO AI TRAINING: Without in any way limiting the author's [and publisher's] exclusive rights under copyright, any use of this publication to "train" generative artificial intelligence (AI) technologies to generate text is expressly prohibited. The author reserves all rights to license uses of this work for generative AI training and development of machine learning language models.

Published by Torrey House Press
Salt Lake City, Utah
www.torreyhouse.org

International Standard Book Number: 978-1-948814-98-0
E-book ISBN: 978-1-948814-99-7
Library of Congress Control Number: 2023936522

Cover art by Tanya Wischerath
Cover design by Kathleen Metcalf
Interior design by Gray Buck-Cockayne
Distributed to the trade by Consortium Book Sales and Distribution

Torrey House Press offices in Salt Lake City sit on the homelands of Ute, Goshute, Shoshone, and Paiute nations. Offices in Torrey are on the homelands of Southern Paiute, Ute, and Navajo nations.

A Wounded Deer – leaps highest –
I've heard the Hunter tell –
'Tis but the Ecstasy of death –
And then the Brake is still!

The Smitten Rock that gushes!
The trampled Steel that springs!
A Cheek is always redder
Just where the Hectic stings!

Mirth is the Mail of Anguish –
In which it Cautious Arm,
Lest anybody spy the blood
And "you're hurt" exclaim!

Emily Dickinson, from *Complete Poems*.
Part One: Life, VIII. 19

"For this land was permeated with dying; this bounteous land, where plants grew overnight, where Jonas had watched a mushroom push from the carcass of a drowned beaver and in a few gliding hours swell to the size of a hat – this bounteous land was saturated with moist and terrible dying."

Ken Kesey, *Sometimes a Great Notion*

Moss River, Oregon

This was a river valley created not by an ambitious god's hands but by the towering mountains acquiescing to the water. Together they made a cradle for giants: giant meadows, giant trees, giant bears. It was always a wet place, deep with water, with sloughs and a wide muddy river that flowed to the north, rich with bogs, creeks, and tributaries. When the rain fell in the Cascade Mountains, it flowed down the western slopes and collected here, and when the rain fell on the east side of the Coast Range, the water flowed down and collected here.

This is the land of skunk and otter and beaver, of mountain lion and red-winged blackbird, red-tailed hawk, golden eagle, sometimes a condor, of wolves—alone and in packs. Their sinewy legs and gleaming teeth are strong beyond comprehension. The trees are colossal; they sway when breathed on by winds from the west or stand towering and still. There are deer, of course. They graze the tall grasses that taste of nutmeg and low clouds and then their tracks disappear into the thick green Everything. At night the frogs and coyotes make a symphony and the sound pulses and echoes throughout this muddy expanse.

Spring looks just like the other seasons: it's wet. The rain falls and falls, cleaning everything. It burrows down and down and down, through dead logs and soil, through mycelium, through stone.

The water will break the rocks. It won't even take that long.

Jade-green buds start to sprout and the color overwhelms. Over on the coast, sea otters slip and turn through the kelp beds which are vast and dense—an impenetrable blue forest. Sharks and whales glide through the outer waters, submerged in dark, cold glory. There are walls of silver fish, schools of them, but this was before walls or schools. Their shiny bodies, specks of brilliant light, dart back and forth, synchronized with each other, with everything. There are people here at the water's many edges. They move with alertness—they are alive! And "alive" means they feel and respond.

This was before white people came. We know this story. Desecration and loss. Power over and against. It didn't have to be like this. So many rules—ships and wagons and homesteads full of rules. Murder and greed and murder and greed. We know this.

But even now, sit still for longer than you think you're capable, and this old world will present itself to you. Wait for the Camaro blasting '90s classic rock to roll past and for the sawmill to stop its saws for the daily lunch break. The workers know it's time to sit and eat by a whistle that sounds just like the scream of a Barn Owl. The kestrels on the fencepost reveal their secrets in high voices, and the trees send their messages late at night when the stars start their lonely glimmering. Stay awake for it.

Get low to the ground. Lay on it.

Take off your clothes and smear your armpits and genitals with mud. Rub the dark clay into the container made by your collarbones. Don't worry about the worms, the beetles, the fungi, the parasites: they're already a part of you, always have been. Let your body be held—flawed, gorgeous, and full of need.

Most of the time we want to live, in spite of everything.

I wake up in the backseat of our car, parked outside a bar called The Night Light, east of Moss River. It's different from the daytime when Mom and I drive to the grocery outlet on Saturday mornings. Tonight the parking lot is full of beat-up cars like ours—no shiny new ones. There's a neon sign that only half works, just the word "Night" flashing and flashing. Music and laughter float out from the door and someone with a deep voice keeps yelling "Lola!" over and over. If I could get out and find Lola, I would ask her why she is so wanted, but Mom said my job is to wait here in the car and not get out—there are bad people all around. The car door needs to stay locked and I hunch low in the seat so no one will know I'm here. Mom can't get in trouble anymore.

My favorite blanket covers me. It's blue with sea turtles and palm trees on it, and my name is stitched in the corner. Smokey Klein, like I wrote it there myself in red thread. On the seat are a plastic water bottle, a bag of oatmeal cookies, and a deck of cards frayed at the edges. Mom taught me how to play Solitaire last year. It's fun if you can keep it going—but once you start losing it's okay to cheat because you're only cheating yourself. The cards fan out on the black vinyl seat, threatening to slip off. The light filtering in from the flashing neon shows I didn't shuffle well.

Mom has a new boyfriend named Jerome. Mom is the manager at the paint factory and Jerome started working there a few weeks ago. When he comes over to hang out with Mom at our house he says things like, "Is your kid going to be hanging around us all night, or what?"

That's when I know to go away.

"Go hide in your rabbit den," Mom whispers lately, and then just mouths the words, *I'm sorry,* so he for sure won't hear.

Jerome mostly wants to be in Mom's bedroom. She's got a futon mattress on the floor and red satin sheets. She's got a stack of magazines and a glass ashtray next to the bed and keeps the curtains closed and the door locked. I am not allowed in, but sometimes I look through the crack if she leaves it open accidentally.

When Jerome comes over, I do not look through the crack. I look at him other times though—I need to know what I'm up against with this one. He has a body like a Grizzly bear, with yellowed teeth and huge, hairy hands. He's got a bald spot on the back of his head and he wears flannel shirts that are too tight. His belt buckle is shiny silver in the shape of a rooster.

"It's a cock," he said when he first caught me admiring it. Mom shushed him and swatted at his shoulder but he just laughed.

Jerome isn't too mean yet, but it usually doesn't take long for a boyfriend to get mean. Some are nicer for a little longer than others. Ernesto was nice for a lot longer than most but then he got mean, too. Sometimes I'm not there for the meanness but there are signs—a hole punched in the wall Mom fixed with white putty and paint while she cried. And once there were bloody bandages in the bathroom after a night of screaming and yelling and pounding thuds. That was the same night I dreamt of hiding in the bushes with a backpack full of poison arrows while an army of men came stumbling like drunkards down the road. I had to hit them right in the chest one by one to keep us safe, and with each arrow shot, another man collapsed in the gravel and crumbled into dust.

Two people come out of the bar, but it's not Mom and Jerome. These ones are walking crooked and don't make it to their own car. They lean against ours instead, not noticing me inside. The woman is pressed against the car and the man is pressing her. They're kissing and it's too wet-sounding and I want to bang on the glass and tell them to get away and go to hell. Finally, the woman says, "Stop TJ, you're hurting me," and then they go off to find their own car. She looks like she doesn't want to go to the other car but she does anyway.

I can't stand waiting here anymore with the "Night" flashing forever. I grab the cookies and the water. I am pretty sure I can find the way home. It won't take too many hours walking and I can cut through the park with the big rock, then maybe take the shortcut under the bridge instead of over it—that could save some time. I leave my blanket even though it's cold—I don't want anyone to see me and think I'm a baby.

The black night sky has sucked up all the sounds and the train tracks are quiet. Last year, one of Mom's old boyfriends showed me how to put my ear and hands to the metal rail. He taught me you can feel a train coming a long time before your eyes can see it coming. He also told me not to flatten pennies on the rail because when a train comes by it could come flying out like a razor blade and slice my face open.

No trains tonight.

Maybe the train conductor is still in bed somewhere, dreaming about all the different sounds metal can make.

I am eight now. Mom sometimes calls me her Easter rabbit because I was born in the spring, but she doesn't believe in Easter and Bible stuff. Some days she says her church is the red-tailed hawks flying in wide circles over the field behind our house, and some days it's the silvery creek that only runs in the spring when the snow melts in the mountains. Other times, her church is a fresh pack of Lucky Strikes, a cold glass of water, and the sun on her face.

My church is in my muscles when I run as hard as I can and the wind makes my hair fly all around and I feel like a wild animal. It's in the old truck tires people dump by the side of our road that fill with water and then, from nothingness, tadpoles appear. My church is when dreams drift down and the night-birds tell me secrets while I sleep.

I reach the park with the big rock and remember the first time Mom brought me here. She needed to get us out of the house because one of her boyfriends was "being unreasonable." Her face was blotched red and she watched me closely as I climbed the ladder and ran around the big rock. She tried to smile when I passed her again but her mouth turned down at the corners.

"You're a scrappy little creature, aren't you?" she said like she was noticing me for the first time.

When I took a rest and sat next to her, she reached out to touch my arm and said she had thought I was going to come out brown when I was born.

"But look here," she said, "You're almost as white as me."

She called it our "German stock" and her lips parted to say more, but instead she closed them tight and felt around in her purse for her Lucky Strikes. All out. People say we look exactly alike but I'll never have long hair and I'll never wear dresses in the summer. I flexed my muscles and ran away from her, imagining the sun browning my skin dark, dark, dark, and turning us into strangers.

I'm at the bridge now. There's a streetlamp lighting the path but it's longer this way. You have to walk around a long chain-link fence to the sidewalk and then walk back on the other side. Then you have to cross the bridge in the crosswalk. Mom told me if I ever cross a street where there's not a crosswalk and get hit by a car I'll be flattened into a pancake and it'll be my fault. Under the bridge would be faster, but it's dark down there, with echoes falling into brown puddles that look too big to jump across.

If Mom and Jerome are still in the bar, maybe they're talking about how lucky they are that I can stay in the car alone so they can have their grown-up time. Or maybe Mom is enjoying herself but wants to come give me a hug and say, "Hi, Little Rabbit. Are you warm enough?"

The only reason she doesn't is that Jerome will be lonely and say to her, "How about one more drink?" but it won't be a question. Even if she doesn't come out, the important thing is she wants to. Later, when she finds the car empty, her face will turn from soft to sharp to scared. I've seen that happen a few times. Will she assume I got kidnapped? Or maybe she will have forgotten me completely; she and Jerome will push their bodies against the car the same way those other people did, not noticing anything important at all.

The bridge. If I run under as fast as I can and out the other side, I'll almost be home. Last year in school we read a book about a troll living under a bridge. It was about two young billy goats who trick the troll into not eating them because they're small and scrawny. When the troll tries to eat the biggest billy goat the goat says, "Well, come along. I've got two spears and I'll poke your eyeballs out your ears." Our teacher used to read us the books we wanted, and everyone always chose that one. I don't have a spear, but the troll probably won't want me because I'm not very meaty—he will wait for a juicy, slow kid to take a short-cut.

I climb down the hill on the side of the road to get under the bridge. There are some broken bottles and the green glass shimmers in the streetlight. Under the bridge though, there's no more light, only the smell of piss and the sound of a car driving on the road above, probably with the windows rolled down because Dolly Parton is blasting from their radio so clearly it's like she's sitting right next to me and singing in my ear. It's her song "9 to 5," but when Mom and I sing it we change it to "8 to 6" because that's how long she works every day filling up paint cans.

There is a troll under the bridge but he's asleep. He's snoring underneath a dirty blanket and his feet are poking out—big, black work boots, untied and caked with mud. My stomach is so tight it's hard to breathe because if he wakes up I'm a goner, but I'm one of the fastest runners in my grade. I breathe in and out and sprint, trying not to make too much noise, jumping across the huge brown puddles and over another bottle before making it to the other side.

Now it's easy—only a darkened gas station, a few more houses, and a trailer park to pass. Our road is thick with oak, cedar, and pine trees, and there are empty lots with sturdy weeds growing up where the cement is busted. There are deer who roam the fields behind our house and there's an owl hooting nearby. Mom taught me the difference between the sound of an owl and the sound of a mourning dove, so I'm sure it's an owl even though it's hidden in the branches. I hoot to her saying, *Thanks for keeping me company,* and she hoots back, *It's too late for you to be out alone.*

At home the back door is unlocked but all the lights are out. Mom and Jerome are still at the bar. I keep all my clothes on except my shoes and socks, still wet from the puddles. I crawl onto my bed on the floor of the narrow closet off the hallway between Mom's room and the bathroom. I want to lie down now—want to lie here until Mom and Jerome come home and ask how I figured out the way back all by myself. Mom will look at me with a lot of emotions on her face and say she is sorry she left me alone for so long. She'll say it won't ever happen again, and she'll mean it.

My eyes are closed now, but sleep won't come. Maybe Mom and Jerome won't ever come back; maybe they'll be so glad I disappeared they'll drive off to live someplace else, someplace better than junky, old Moss River with all its rain and cold and mud and bars and busted-up chain-link fences. They won't even come back to get their stuff because they'll be so excited to be free from all this. They'll head someplace with beautiful houses and no weeds and no rain once they think I'm gone for good. This is the loneliness that finally pushes me under—this is the beginning of my new life alone.

Mom and I are sitting under the fig tree behind our small blue house. The back steps are held up with cement blocks because they're rotting, and there are ferns growing up from underneath. The gutters have plants growing in them, too—once I even saw some yellow flowers up there.

It's the first warm day of the year and sweat trickles down my sides, soaking the elastic band of my corduroy pants. We sit in old lawn chairs someone left on the side of the road. When we brought them home Mom said we had done a good job by recycling them. The straps will break soon, but for now their yellow and green stripes hold us in the air, and we lean back with the sun on our faces, finally.

The fig tree takes up most of our yard, its branches spreading out like the jungle canopy we read about in Ms. O'Brien's class. She showed us pictures of leaves bigger than our desks and wide-eyed monkeys hidden in the branches. Our fig tree is bright green with sparrows and squirrels, and every once in a while a family of deer come through and nibble off all the leaves they can reach. One scrapes his antlers against the lowest branches, and his thick, gray coat is dull against the vibrance around him. The others are smaller, nimbler, moving through the brambles soundlessly, attuned to everything.

Mom gets a certain look sometimes. Kind of scared but like she's ready for any kind of fight. Beneath this green shade and warmth, she has that look now—her lips tremble but her jaw is hard-set. She tells me my father was named Paul Thomas. As she starts to talk, a breeze comes through, cooling us, and the green shadows flicker across her face. The wind has come to comfort her, but she is concentrating too much on what she wants to get off her chest to feel anything else.

Last week, Ms. O'Brien told my second-grade class we were going to be making Father's Day cards before school let out for the summer. My non-existent father hadn't been on my mind much before; lots of people don't have dads, or they wish they didn't. My friend Toby, with his jet-black hair, pale skin, and a gap between his big teeth, lives across the road and has plans to stab his dad to death with a long, rusty screwdriver we found in the back field. He brushed dirt from metal and held it like a spear—lunging and stabbing the cool, evening air with determination. It's hidden under his mattress now for when the time comes.

Mom looks up at the hard, green figs and the light filters down. She is young, I know that. Her skin is smooth and tender—no wrinkly leather-arms like Mrs. Lorrie who monitors recess for the kindergarteners. Mom says that not too long before I was born, she had been in love with Paul, but he stopped returning her calls.

"I was only nineteen years old when I got pregnant," she tells me. "I didn't understand anything about love or how things worked. And I was desperate for attention. I was lonely."

I don't say anything and concentrate as hard as I can. I know she needs me to listen.

"After he stopped coming around and I had already started dating someone else is when I found out you were growing inside me," she continues, rubbing her deflated belly. "I didn't know what to do. I wasn't sure what the right thing was."

She made the decision to let me keep getting stronger—

tap-tapping inside her with my knees and elbows whenever she put on Stevie Wonder records.

Mom reaches out her arms for a hug and says she needs to get started making dinner. As quickly as it started, our conversation is over—clouds rolled in while she told me about Paul and being young and not knowing anything, and now it's starting to drizzle, flecks of cooling silver streaking the windows as I follow Mom into the house. I retreat to my bed and fill up sheets of lined paper with my father's name.

Paul Thomas. Paul Thomas. Paul Thomas.

I scrawl it over and over until my hand cramps, trying to make him real, but am interrupted by a knock outside my closet. The smell of grilled chicken follows behind Mom as she opens the door a crack.

"I'm so sorry," Mom tells me. "I lied."

I poke my head out and the ceiling light in the living room flickers like we have a ghost. I watch a small fly bang itself against the glass globe trying to get free, but every attempt is an injury to eye and wing.

"Your biological father, your real dad, is Danny—Daniel Washington. I dated him around the same time things were ending with Paul. Danny was sweet but I was more attached to Paul, always wanted him to come back. I wanted to somehow make it so Paul was your father, at least in our minds. But, he's not. The timing just isn't right and you look nothing like Paul. I'm sorry I lied. I'm not good at this."

I'm not sure what she is good at or not good at. And what is a name, anyways?

A week later, Mom opens up her purse with a grin to show me a big wad of extra gas money. I don't know exactly what it means until we are packed into the car with pillows and snacks and driving through the Old Cedar Corridor, a dark forest west of town, and then beyond even that. We emerge from those thick trees at the gray-blue Pacific—on a makeshift vacation where we sleep curled up in our Volkswagen Beetle at an unlit rest stop, huddled into Snoopy sleeping bags we got on sale at Kmart, playing Crazy 8's, and putting in quarters for hot chocolate from the graffitied vending machine.

The next day at the Oregon Coast Center—standing near the black and white photographs of lighthouses and fishermen and logging trucks sliding into Satan's Bath—the smell of salt hangs in the air from the crashing waves, and I ask for a new name.

"Mom," I start, staring at the sea captains' hard faces in black and white, their woolen caps pulled down over their ears, "Can I change my name to Rocky?"

When she turns to me, I understand I should have waited for another time to ask, but it is too late now. Her answer is clear before she speaks, told by the way her shoulders tighten, in the way her jaw sets, clenched like a tight grip.

"Absolutely not," she says. "You may not change your name to Rocky. Your name is one of the only positive things I've given you."

She leaves me standing there and goes to look at an exhibit on the history of Oregon coast shark attacks. I watch her go, her faded blue jeans worn out and too loose on her body, dark brown hair trailing behind her, wild like a horse's tail.

I want to explain all the pushups I've been doing, the pretend boxing, setting my pillow up to look like a man's broad chest, and punching it first thing in the morning before Mom knows I am awake, like I am in the ring, and everyone is cheering. I want the toughness and the hardness of stones, boulders even, an avalanche. Rocky.

The huge telescopes set up outside on the deck are pointed down to the darkened water below. It crashes over and over against the black rocks, but then a gray body emerges, a small sea lion. Through the telescope, his whiskers twitch. He looks right at me, lifts a flipper, and waves—*Don't worry*, he mouths, his whiskers and sharp teeth glinting in the afternoon sun, *Everything is going to be okay.*

In the backseat on the way home I write my chosen name in a growing stack of secret notes I keep tucked into the cracked vinyl of the back seat. The ancient trees out the window watch us pass and shake their mossy arms at us. Back at our house, when the car is unpacked and Mom says she needs some time alone, Toby crosses the road in his bare feet and promises to call me Rocky when our moms aren't around.

Rocky Washington. Rocky Washington. Rocky Washington.

When the rain makes it too wet to sit under our fig tree, Mom tells me things at the kitchen table, one part of the story at a time. A flighty bird, she brings in stems from outside—pine branches, willow stalks, and the tiny, white flowers that grow almost year-round. She places them in water and tends to them with quick hands, little claw fingers.

Today the rain won't let up; dark storm clouds are resting above the mossy tree line, and she has that look.

"Danny, your dad, was Black, so I wasn't sure what color you would be."

"Because of our German stock?" I ask, and her eyebrows come together like she's thinking too hard.

"I thought you were too young to remember that," she says, "But yes. At first you had very thick black hair. Later it laid down, flattened to these loose curls."

She reaches out to touch my head, but I duck and weave like the real Rocky, tired of these big talks, this heavy seesaw rising and falling beneath me.

"Danny and I only dated for a couple of months," she continues. "He was quiet and shy, and lived in an attic in northeast Portland with some other boys who had come back from Vietnam all messed up in the head."

She hesitates but decides to keep going.

"They used heroin to try to stay calm after all the things

they saw and did over there. It was like a medicine they needed. I tried it with them once, but Danny had to put the needle in for me. I might have done it more, but I hated that cold sharpness—it made me nauseous and anyways, it was warmth I was after. Danny taught me helpful things, too—how to make hash browns, how to dance to Cuban music, and how to get free bread from behind the bakery on 23rd Ave. He was nice enough, but I was still in love with Paul. I do have a picture though, of Danny when he was a boy about your age. Want me to get it?"

Danny Washington. Danny Washington. Danny Washington.

She takes a thick book off the top shelf above where I can reach and opens it in the middle, pulling out a folded snapshot of a brown, mischievous face framed by an ironed shirt with a soft, white collar.

"We look the same," I say, amazed by his small, familiar body, stomach-sick because she hasn't shown me sooner—even in this way, I've missed out on knowing him.

I run to the bathroom mirror, hold the photograph next to my face, and peer into our shared reflection for clues.

This changes everything. Mom found this old picture but I'm the one who has been found—I'm looking at him and he's looking back at me, too. He's telling his older self all about me, with our identical almond-shaped eyes and dark eyebrows. Mom doesn't look happy about having gotten all this off her chest. The ground under me is just like the quicksand on Saturday morning cartoons except I'm the one sinking now.

Mom's confessions are sometimes followed by a dark cloud, and somehow I know the storm coming is my fault. With her truth-tellings can come unexpected backhands—for mistakes I made, for crying too much, for being too quiet, too unresponsive, for being "so fucking difficult." She doesn't like it when I react, even if my reaction is not reacting; she wants to be the one with the big feelings. A few days ago, she reached out to wipe crumbs off my cheek—a gentle gesture—but I flinched at her touch. My whole body turned afraid of her and she knew it. She pulled her hand back and curled into herself, weeping into her palms and apologizing.

"I'm so sorry. I'm so sorry."

She feels so awful, I doubt she will hit me again, but I no longer want her touch in other ways either. I haven't run to give her hugs when she picks me up from the YMCA after school. I haven't rubbed her tight shoulders when she comes home from work. And I haven't let her wash my hair like she used to. I am learning something about touch and power, of giving and taking away, and my experiment isn't over.

Mom leaves to go get milk and Lucky Strikes at Rajesh's Market. I like going with her, but today she says she needs a minute alone, that she'll be right back. Mr. Rajesh is about two hundred years old. When he smiles his eyes shine bright like a little kid's, even though his face has the deepest wrinkles I've ever seen. Mr. Rajesh is an ancient tortoise, moving slow, but sometimes he still manages to sneak a hard piece of Bazooka out of a jar to give to me without Mom even noticing.

With her at Rajesh's without me, I go into her bedroom, sliding across the floor in sock feet. It makes sense she doesn't want me to come in when a man is there, but I don't know why she doesn't want me to visit in the quiet times either. She told me not to come in or even knock when her door is closed unless something extra terrible happens—

"Terrible like...you cut off your finger," she had said. "If there's no blood anywhere you can handle it like a Big Kid until I come out."

The turquoise earrings on her dresser are gathering dust, and her clothes are folded in their drawers. In her closet are dresses she never wears, and work boots—no pretty shoes anymore; they all busted. The only painting on the wall used to be in the living room. She told me she made it in her high school art class.

"It's a self-portrait," she told me, but it's of a brown rabbit. The rabbit stands on its hind legs in a field, wears a blue jacket, and looks toward something off in the distance.

Her bed is messy, with only one pillow. I wonder who gets the pillow when a man is here. Does she give it to him or do they share? I don't think she'd take it for herself. I lay my head on it, pretend I'm a man spending the night for the first time, and look out at the cold room. How would it feel?

Under the pillow there's a book, but not a regular book. It's got empty pages in the back and Mom's handwriting in the front. Her hard loops and lines. There aren't many pages filled up, but they go back a long time. I try to picture Mom in here writing alone. Maybe she does it when I'm asleep. Maybe this is why I'm not allowed in. I wonder if she lets her boyfriends read what she writes or if it's just for her. I flip to the first page.

> I haven't kept a journal since senior year of high school. In a way this kind of writing seems childish to me, but Angela says it helps her get clearer in her mind, helps her know why she does the things she does and what to do next, what to focus on. I could use that. I know I'm doing it all wrong, or at least most of the time. Today Smokey started speaking again. I should have gone straight to the doctor when it happened, not just tried to fix everything myself like usual. I have to remember it's not just me any-more—this little person is completely reliant on me for everything—sometimes I forget and sometimes it's all I think about. Forget and remember, forget and remember. There are two of us now and the weight of this is something I never imagined. I'm just so fucking tired. Baby years were easier because Smokey's wants and needs were the same things, and I knew what to do so instinctively. But with age, things have gotten more confusing because my needs—even my wants—matter too. All I know is I want to do better. I feel so alone and lonely but I want to get this one thing right.

—

I hear our car pull into the driveway. Mom has the radio on and the sound floats over everything as I put the book back under her pillow and take one more look around the room, making sure I didn't do anything to give myself away.

On PBS there's a nature show with a man's voice telling us about the mother gazelle, the mother orangutan, and the mother eagle, and how they are all hungry or dying or suffering in different kinds of ways—and mostly about how they are about to be killed. This man stays calm as he tells us this, as if he is explaining all this pain from very far away. The predator is going to kill them all, and sometimes the predator is a human—a human man. Mostly though, there is a chase, across vast hills or along silty waterways or in the sky, and in the chase you see glossy blackness—raw fear—surrounded by the whites of eyes.

The music gets louder on the TV and that's when you know the mother animal is about to be killed—her babies will be left alone to suffer for a while and then they'll probably be killed, too. The man on the TV tells us this is just the way the world works. The beautiful elephant with her tusks hacked off while she's still alive—he finds it interesting.

The gazelle always goes limp in the lion's mouth, and later the man's camera shows us her bloodied, white rib cage burning in the desert sun. Over and over and over and over and over he says, *It's just the rules of nature.*

Beyond our fig tree and past the wooden fence that has almost rotted away, covered in moss and ivy and returning to dirt, is a family of oak trees, then train tracks for freight cars, then a migrant camp, then more trees, and then I'm not sure what comes after that—I've never gone that far. The migrant camp smells sour sometimes or thick with something too-sweet and rotten, but when Mom and I walked back there once a long time ago she said it's not their fault—there aren't any toilets or wooden homes with real walls because America is run by capitalistic fascists. "Fash-ists," she said slowly for me, so I would remember the word for later.

Sometimes I sit against the bark of this one old oak tree, far enough away that the people at the camp won't know I'm there because I'm small and don't make any sounds, but close enough that I can watch them in the distance if I squint. Nothing much happens. There is often the sound of a guitar coming from the tents or the campfire and once I heard bottles breaking, but usually it is quiet. Mom says it's a place for eating and resting between shifts, showering with the rainwater they collect in old cattle troughs, and maybe looking at the stars on clear nights before they give in to heavy sleep.

The first time I went to the back field alone was when Mom was busy with one of her boyfriends in her room. I had spent the morning in the living room waiting for her door to open, for her to say, "Good morning," and give me a hug, but she wasn't coming out.

I went to the field to get away from the moaning sounds leaking out from under the door like something wet and spilled. The rain from the night before made everything glimmer, dripping from the pine needles and falling hard. At the last fence, I pulled up the barbed wire and crawled through. On the other side I stood up—face to face with a young deer, one of the smaller ones from the family I'd watched before. She had black eyes and swirls of brown in her fur and ears moving back and forth like leaves in the wind, hearing every breath and sound. Her body twitched and rippled, and her dark nose glistened with wetness. Her legs were thin but strong, a darker color than the rest of her from walking through the tall grasses. I asked her if she was the one who has been nibbling our fig tree leaves. I told her we didn't mind, that she could eat all the leaves she could reach if she wanted—just to leave us a few figs. Her animal smell was warm dirt and fresh rain and blackberry leaves. I wanted to get closer.

With her dark nose twitching, she decided to talk. *You have black pools for eyes like me.*

Then her mother stepped out from behind Old Oak, a twig snapped, and they both turned and bounded away over the tall grasses—hooved flying creatures. If they wanted, they could soar into the clouds, but they prefer the earth to the sky, just like the rain that won't stop falling. They moved down the hill and out of view as the storm front eased up, leaving behind only the smell of rich, clean soil. When I made it back home, Mom and her boyfriend were taking a shower. The hot steam came out from under the door just as their animal noises had—a magic potion wasted—this time floating up and away.

—

Deer is bigger now but still stays with her mom. I don't know where the rest of their family has gone—only these two remain. She talks to me when I go to the field alone, and if I stay very still, Deer and her mother don't go running away from me. If Deer eats some blackberry leaves, I do too. When she lowers her head to reach some new grasses sprouting low, I also get low to the ground and see what I can find.

At our house, the roof sighs under the weight of blackened rain clouds, and we have buckets set up to catch two leaks. Below us, a family of raccoons has moved out of the fields to live underneath our floorboards. The landlord must have seen them move in because he told Mom he was "going to take care of them."

We call him Mean Landlord because he bangs on the door if the rent is late by one day and once we saw him throw his hammer through a window when our neighbor did something that upset him. I try to imagine him—pale and hairy and over six feet tall, an Oregon Sasquatch with his hard scowl and missing teeth—taking care of the raccoons, carefully giving them meat scraps until the babies can make it on their own. Maybe he even lets them sleep in his bed, so they stay warm and dry. Maybe the Mean Landlord isn't so mean after all, but a clump of worry pulses in my stomach and I know I can't trust him to take care of the raccoons. It will be up to me to keep them safe.

These babies poke their twitching noses out from under the porch and wash their faces with their bony, black hands. Sometimes if there aren't any other human sounds, I can hear them under the house talking to each other, discussing all their plans in whispers, deciding who is doing what for chores.

Above their world, inside our house, cigarette smoke fills the living room—Mom is lighting a fresh one off the one that's about to die—and the buckets have to be emptied out and set back in the right spot every couple of hours. Outside, some of the ripe figs we didn't get around to picking are rotting on the ground.

No one wants them now—not Deer, not the squirrels, not the birds, and not the raccoons. Mom puts on rain boots and goes out with clippers to cut dark stems of rosemary. She comes back and places the cuttings in an old Coke bottle and fills it with tap water. When she blows the smoke out of her lungs, she tilts her head way back and looks at me out of the corner of her eye without blinking. The knot in her throat moves as she swallows. Then my own throat tightens because these are the signs something is coming.

"You were molested when you were five," she says, her voice flat and guarded.

I know what that word means but also don't—someone did something shameful and that someone might be me. I watch a honeybee banging himself against the window pane, trying to get out—no one wants to be here. Mom's cigarette smoke curls up toward the ceiling in a spiral—a small tornado winding itself up into nothingness.

"I left you at home with my boyfriend Richard," she tells me in a strange, low voice like it's hard for her to breathe. "I thought I could trust him."

I can barely remember anything about Richard, only his white-blond hair and pale, blue eyes and how I called him *White Richard* when he wasn't listening.

"When you talk about him, I picture a wizard, using all his magic for bad," Toby had said when I mentioned him once. That's when Toby and I first became friends, laughing easily at our own joke about something real—not a knock-knock, not a riddle.

The only other blond person with blue eyes I've seen up close is a red-faced girl who has a stutter and wears the same dirty, plaid dress to school every day.

Mom tells me she had gone to Rajesh's to pick up something we could eat for dinner but came back sooner than expected because she'd forgotten her purse.

"When I got back the bathroom door was locked, and Richard was in there with you. I called out at first, but no one answered. I banged on the door with my fists as hard as I could, then started screaming and kicking and he finally let you out. But it had been minutes. It had been forever. You were a ghost of yourself and wouldn't say anything—you kept looking down, and I knew, I knew..."

She tells me I didn't talk to anyone except her for almost a year after that, but I don't remember my silent year. She says she didn't call the police or the doctor because she was worried I'd be taken away from her by CPS and nothing would happen to Richard anyways—it would all be for nothing.

"Men always get away with it," she says. "The pigs in their blue suits with their shiny guns don't help women and kids, don't forget that—even if they smile and seem nice."

She runs her hand through her hair, massages the back of her neck.

"So. I knew I was on my own—I got rid of Richard and kept trying to love you back to yourself again, and after a while, it worked."

She smiles a weak smile, wanting reassurance—for me to know how hard she tried—how she protected me even when it meant losing a boyfriend. I have already left the room and am floating above the table with this new information, looking down at the tops of our dark heads. I've only just started learning how to float up from the bad things. Had White Richard changed me? What might I have said in my too-quiet year? What words were lost?

I hover up by the ceiling and then higher past the roof and above the treetops toward the stars—maybe this thing with White Richard is why I want to be a boy, someone tougher, more impenetrable. Why I want to be Rocky, why I sometimes pee standing up when I can get away with it, why I steal *Boys'*

Life magazines from the school library because they think I'm a girl and wouldn't understand. Maybe it's White Richard's fault I always want to hit things like the other boys in my grade do—hit things with hockey sticks, baseball bats, with croquet mallets, open hands, with fists. Maybe this is why I want to copy Lisa and have a boyfriend. Lisa is only two grades older, but sometimes she and Alex kiss after school when the teachers are too tired to keep track of us because all they want is to go home. In the afternoons leading up to summer vacation, Ms. O'Brien was always rubbing her temples and looking like she might start crying. Toby told me that on the last day of school, Lisa rubbed Alex's penis in the janitor's closet with the lights off, but he might have made it up.

I've been passing notes and cheap candy from the 7-11 to Tyler who sits behind me in class—not because I want to hold hands or kiss him, but because Tyler and Alex and all the other boys have what I want and I need to get closer to get it, to understand it and make it mine. I need to study them up close—to find out for myself if my boy-ness came before White Richard, or if he made it so—a quick, mean magic trick from behind a locked bathroom door.

When I stop floating up, I'm not thinking about White Richard or the boys at school or any of it; all that exists is my own breathing and my stomach—pulsing with a dull ache like I'm cut and bruised on the inside and it's too wet in there for scabs to stick. Mom is still saying something—her words come out from far away—but somehow I can hear the raccoon family under the house clearly. The parents are handing out the food they've found for the children, seeds and nuts, and maybe some crickets. They're joking around and making plans for tomorrow. My stomach clenches up into a big fist and the pain of it is how I know I'm back on Earth in my body and sitting in the kitchen again. The smell of freshly-cut rosemary smells like medicine.

Mom can tell I'm tired now and rubs the deepening crease between her eyebrows. "If you ever remember anything and want to talk about it, tell me. But for now, this isn't something you should tell anyone else."

She looks at me closely, knows I'm tired out from all my floating away, and leans over to put the back of her hand on my forehead to check if I have a fever. She leads me to the couch and wraps me up with blankets, sets up my favorite movie on our old VCR player that only works sometimes. I choose *Paper Moon*, where the mom is dead and it's hard to convince the dad to stay.

"Your mom's so pretty," Tyler had told me in the morning, when Mom dropped me off at the YMCA for summer camp so she could still get all her hours at work.

"She's not my mom," I replied through squinted eyes, daring him to call me a liar. "She takes care of our garden sometimes. She knows a lot about plants."

Kaleb Blackgoat comes to us from his tribal land on the other side of the mountain range on the weekends. When he walks through our house, he has to bow down so his forehead doesn't smack into the door frames—he's that tall. I've never known a man with a braid before, but he has a thick black one that swings from the nape of his neck—a weighted rope. If I fell off a cliff, Kaleb is the kind of person who might reach out his long arms to help, he might yell down for me to hold on tight. He would pull me up and give me a hug and tell me to be more careful, but he wouldn't be mad, just worried. When he speaks to us, his voice is deep and low. He is quiet and calm, settling into our house and smelling like something softer than tobacco smoke—piñon and sweetgrass.

Kaleb is different from Mom's other boyfriends—he doesn't want to hurt anyone, and he laughs more, though he is often serious, too. Mom's boyfriends are never my friends but maybe Kaleb could be. I wait on the orange couch near the front window and keep a lookout, watch for his car to pull up—a beat-to-hell silver Ford Fairlane with a loose muffler and black, furry dice hanging from the rearview. When he walks in, it doesn't matter the weather—sometimes the windows are cracked open to let a breeze in and sometimes it is cold enough for our breath to hang there all ghostly—the first thing he does is take off his shirt, revealing his massive torso. It holds pockmarks and unsettling scars that run in all directions in ragged lines. I watch his body, curious about the things it has done and the things that have been done to it, as he lays face down on the carpeted floor and calls me over. Kicking off my shoes and socks, my job is to walk all over his back—an offering, a token, a makeshift healing. My narrow feet slide over his tight skin, feeling the raised marks. It is hard to stay on without falling off—toes and heels digging in, a game to get better at—his ribs rising and falling with each deep breath.

He always pats me on the shoulder afterward.

"Thanks, kiddo," he says with a low laugh for what he calls *Smokey's World Famous Rental Carpet Massage,* then leaves for the kitchen where Mom is waiting. Even though I like Kaleb, their kissing mouths sound awful—a strange, desperate pact—a promise that maybe will or maybe won't be kept.

When we eat dinner, Kaleb includes me in the conversation and asks me questions about things. Tonight he asks me what I thought about living in a place where it rains so much, and it's the first time I really understand it might be possible to live somewhere different. Even Ms. O'Brien's tropical jungle was wet with rain dripping off the desk-sized leaves and ropey vines.

"I don't ever want to leave my trees and animals," I say and he doesn't laugh or look at Mom with a funny expression, like they're in on something and I'm the one left out. He nods in agreement and eats the stew Mom made. He tells her thank you and that it tastes real good. Mom rests her hand on his arm because everything in our house is easy now.

Sometimes when they're in the bedroom with the door closed, instead of banging a pot or kicking the door to make them come out and remember I'm here, I pretend to be asleep on the living room couch, holding myself as still as I can. I want them to come out of the room and find me there—to hear them say to each other I'm special and I matter—I want to mean something to them. I try to make myself look easy to love—a carefully wrapped-up present they'd be delighted to find. I concentrate on staying still, hoping Kaleb will pick me up and take me to my closet bed with his enormous arms, lifting me up with more sureness than is possible with Mom's thin arms and bony bird shoulders. When he does lift me, exactly as I had hoped, I let my head sink into his wide chest and smell his warm smell, working hard to keep my muscles relaxed, my eyes closed and my breath steady. I want to make this feeling last.

Back in my bed, their voices carry through the thin closet wall, saying some white men, grave robbers, have stolen some things belonging to the tribe, and Kaleb and a friend of his are going to make it right. Their voices start to fade, and I dream of a vast green cemetery. I want to tell him the cedar trees will help keep them safe and hidden, tell him I hope they make it.

Things have been different since the night of my listening through the wall. Mom tells me she and Kaleb are breaking up. Usually, I'm glad when a boyfriend gets broken up with, but I don't want Kaleb to go—he is the best one she's ever found. Kaleb's leaving happens without any of the usual fighting and door-slamming from Mom's other break-ups. She tells me Kaleb is being pressured by his tribe to not date white women. Mom says this as she sets dirty dishes into the sink and explains how Kaleb knows how to be kind and gentle, not only for a moment but for the whole time—and how rare that is for a man. Tears leak out of her eyes as she places her soapy hands on the counter, then she slams a plate into the sink so hard it shatters into blue shards, and I leave to go sit on the orange couch alone.

No one asked me if I wanted to give one more rental carpet massage or to say goodbye at all. Across the kitchen is stale bread left out on the counter, past the hallway to the bedroom are Mom's faded sheets in a heap, and in the living room there is Mom, walking away from the slivers of glass left behind her in the sink. She sits with her defeated eyes closed and an unlit cigarette about to fall through her fingers. I look down at my own light skin, the same color as hers, and don't understand how it has taken him away from us, how it has made our one good man leave.

The raccoons are gone, too, and I let myself believe it was Kaleb who took them. I imagine them climbing into his Ford one by one to be driven away from all these crazy white people to a dark green forest where they can live better lives, far from the Mean Landlord and all the other dangers here.

After crying alone in her room for a few hours, Mom comes out and tells me to put on my shoes. She wants to take me somewhere. We drive past empty lots and trailer parks to where all the big stores in town sit—cement boxes lined up in cement parking lots. She looks at me, but I just look at my hands. I thought she was going to drive us west through the forest all the way to the coast where Kaleb lives, hoped that she had an idea about how to get him to come back to us, to keep making things feel so right. She can tell I don't want to be here—I don't understand why we are shopping right now, but then she gets me out of the car and pulls me along to the pet section, where I am almost never allowed to go.

There are hamsters in cramped cages and birds flapping their wings against tight bars and Mom says she "can't fucking stand all this torture, all this pain," and I can't either. The rabbit babies have a slightly bigger pen but choose to all stay together in a tight huddle under the bright lights. Their dark eyes don't even blink. Mom tells me to pick whichever one I want.

"This one isn't going to live in a cage," she tells me, and I want to take all of them home but finally choose a little black one who looks the most scared. He's slightly apart from the huddle. He's been left out and one of his ears is bent at an angle. He easily fits in my two hands and his heart beats against my fingertips— his neck smells of hay and piss.

When we get him home Mom asks what we should call him and I decide on Moonshadow because we've been playing Cat Stevens records over and over for months. Kaleb liked that song, too, and sometimes he and Mom swayed in the living room together while the record spun and it wasn't sexy and gross—it felt nice they were happy, smiling and relaxing into each other like a secret spell.

When we get home, we set up an area in the backyard where Moonshadow can safely run around in the grass and feel the dew and the sun under the big sky. Inside, he can nibble on my old picture books and stretch out by the heater when it's cold. Mom says to save his little, round shits because they will help next year's vegetable garden grow. She has brightened—both of us petting little Moonshadow as she talks about planting corn, green beans, and maybe even some blueberry bushes—and gives me a hug. Maybe everything is going to be okay, even with Kaleb gone.

"I'm going out with Angela tonight," she says. "Will you and Moonshadow be okay for a couple hours?"

This is new too, this asking to leave. Sometimes after my bedtime she tiptoes out without saying anything and shuts the door quietly, forgetting the rumble of our Volkswagen's engine has always rattled the whole neighborhood. She thinks I'm still a deep sleeper, like I was as a baby, before all the worries came. I've tried staying awake, listening until the sound of our car return- ing fills up the silence—back home to me from wherever she's gone—but usually I can't. I wish she didn't need to leave but I have Moonshadow to keep me company now, and I nod my yes.

With the house so quiet and an emptiness creeping up the

walls, I still don't want to accept Kaleb isn't coming back. He was wanted here by both of us. We agreed on him in our own way and I imagined him in our lives for longer, thought maybe he'd drive me to school in the fall when it rained, hailed, or snowed too hard. All the kids would ask me if he was my dad and I'd tell them yes. I thought there'd be more nights of him helping Mom with the dishes, something other boyfriends never did. It made her happy, his huge hands all soapy and sure while she leaned in the doorway, watched him, and laughed easily.

Mom's been gone a few hours and the neighborhood is dark and still, no owls tonight. Moonshadow goes to his shoebox of hay to go to bed—he's had a big day and misses the other rabbits. I pet his soft, black fur and tell him he is safe here. After a while, I get up and walk to the living room to balance on the couch's worn-out armrests in the dark—faded orange velvet about to rip open from wear. I pretend it is my job to stay on—to stay steady here in this place, as strong and calm as Kaleb had been—no matter what.

Sunset on the river means all the insects come, right before everything goes dark. The stink from the mushroom canning factory up the road makes my eyes water in the daytime but blows away as evening comes and the winds pick up. Even the semi-trucks that pass on their way from the fields to I-5 moan out a slow grumble like they too are tired. Mom is in the kitchen steaming artichokes. She leans over the silver pot of steam, says she's at the kitchen spa for the best facial around.

"Look outside Smokey," she says, pointing into the dusty evening. "The sky's the exact color of a blood orange."

We both stand there, our faces lit up by the warm-red ending of the day, quiet in our own thoughts. Things have been better with us lately—no hits at all, and I've started hugging her again, letting myself relax into her familiar body. It's best when she makes big, lazy circles on my back as I fall asleep, or ruffles my hair when she passes in the hall. Mom will be changing into fresh clothes soon, because her new boyfriend Claudio is coming over, but she still has on her shirt and jeans from work.

She has a new job cutting gloves at the leather warehouse along the river—ten hours of heavy, metal scissors following the outline of five fingers—gloves others will wear for protection, while her own hands become raw and stiff in the making of them. She is twenty-eight and I am eight, and she tells me those twenty years between us are our lucky number. When we play the lottery, we always start with the number twenty.

"That was the number of years I was here on Earth without you," she often says, and though she does her best to love me, the way she says it makes it clear something has been lost.

Claudio has puffy skin like he's been taken fresh from the oven, and his face is round and smooth. It's easy to imagine him as a boy even though he has a pillowy gut from cases of beer and his breath smells of yeast. He tries to hide his smell with the Shulton's Old Spice he leaves in our bathroom, which stinks up the whole house even when he's not around. He works the hop fields in late spring and summer until harvest starts in August, and picks strawberries and pears, too. At other times of the year he does odd jobs around town.

He is from Guadalajara and he tells stories of his family there, his time as a kid growing up.

"No one there had nothing. Nothing at all," he tells us tonight while Mom rolls hamburger into meatballs. "And my mother," he says, with a mix of both pride and shame, "is so tall people say she is a transvestite."

Moonshadow darts behind the couch, a black dustball skidding across the floor. He doesn't like Claudio and hides under or behind things when he is around, unlike other times when he stretches out at our bare feet or lays on the old wooden floorboards, warming himself up when there's a splash of light.

"But no," Claudio says after a long silence in which he remembers something else, "she just has a strong jawline. And she for sure has a pussy."

He laughs a low, rumbly laugh and wants to know if he's gone too far, if he has succeeded in being shocking. He hasn't been around long enough to understand it is difficult to surprise either one of us. *Pussy, pussy, pussy*—that's nothing. There have been so many others before him, a long tornado of men coming up our road and staggering in, wrecking things, and spinning back out. We've *been around the block*, as Mom likes to say—a thing to be proud of.

A few months ago, at the gas station, we were waiting for our turn at the pump in our Volkswagen. The metal of the car is so eroded I can watch the road pass by underneath me through the floorboards like the Flintstones. The gas station attendant was young with tan skin and smiling eyes and as he started walking over to our car, he burst into flames, easy, like the flick of a lighter. The gas pump nearest him did, too. Mom screamed and covered my eyes. Then she got out to help but by then other people were there and running inside to call an ambulance. She returned to the car out of breath and we drove away, over the curb and out of there.

"Did he light a match or something?" I asked.

Once, behind the mushroom canning factory, a boy with a bruised neck and jaw had poured gasoline from a plastic milk jug onto the dirt and threw a match. The whole thing whooshed up in hot flames so fast the hair on his arms got singed. He showed us his arms after, laughing, but all I could smell was his burnt fur.

Mom ignored my question, reached for a cigarette to calm her nerves, then thought better of it and shoved the pack back under her seat.

Sometimes still, behind my eyes in unexpected moments, there is the burning gas station boy, coming toward us with his kind face.

For this and other reasons, when Claudio tells us about his tall, manly mother and her pussy, we lean back and listen, taking it in. Anytime he's had a few beers he tells the story over and over again, as if he's stuck in it, or wants us to figure something out about who he is and where he comes from. Sometimes Mom doesn't quite know what to make of Claudio but she isn't surprised by him.

"I once dated someone who lied about having served in Korea," Mom tells him. "He was a lot older than me and made up excuses for all his fucked-up behavior. I wish he hadn't punched in all the walls in the bedroom. Remember him, babe?"

She looks at me and gives me her full attention for a moment. That boyfriend had deep wrinkles in his face like cracked earth, and had punched the walls, punched Mom, and punched me, but she leaves those last parts out. He watched football and smoked cigars—filled up the air in the house with his own special kind of poison—and had scabs on his fleshy knuckles because of his temper. Even if it's a bad memory, I get a secret thrill when Mom includes me in her adult conversations.

It's dark outside now and two owls are hooting to each other. Beyond their calls, the rumble of trucks on the highway sounds the same as the ocean—each truck driver is a boy in a boat, either trying to get away from home or trying to get back. Mom has made spaghetti for dinner and lets me throw a noodle against the wall above the stove to make sure it is cooked all the way through. It hangs there like a worm, then flops to the floor trying to escape.

At the table I push the food around on my plate, trying to focus on the conversation. The noodles are all worms now, wishing they were back in the dirt. Mom says I should eat more because I need to grow up to be strong and tall. I haven't been able to eat much lately. There's a mouth in my stomach with sharp little teeth, and when things are scary around me, the teeth start chomping. If there's no food, the teeth give up and the mouth closes and we can get along okay. Things that put the teeth to sleep: warm milk, being alone, no boyfriends, Moonshadow, going outside, listening to birds, and watching storm clouds change shape. They like when the fog rolls out and everything turns a brighter shade of green, glistening in the moisture. The teeth wake up hungry around Claudio, even when he's talking in his normal voice, not doing anything scary. I take my noodles to the kitchen and put them back in the pot and stir them around with the leftovers and no one notices.

Claudio keeps going with his story, tells us his mother's name is Veronica, and on their street back in Guadalajara, everyone called him *El Mamoncito*. He was a momma's boy and he used to get beat up, he tells us, pausing to let that sink in, as if it's hard to imagine. Even now, all big and strong, he looks like an enormous baby, slumped in his chair, drinking his beer, and spitting out the sunflower seeds he always eats after dinner. I wouldn't mind calling him *El Mamoncito* and punching him myself. I picture my fist sinking into his gut and wonder if he would even notice. Claudio tells us how before he crossed the border, Veronica told him his father was a rough, beautiful man who had traveled the country hopping trains, *como un romantico*. She said he was a singer, a passionate love-maker, and not the type to stay in one place, with one person.

Veronica explained to him that he got his father's handsome looks, but she hoped he wouldn't be the kind of man to run away from the people who need him.

Claudio tells Mom all this and then admits he's not sure what type of man he is and looks at her, but she isn't too concerned with Claudio being the type to run away or not. She's not too needy with Claudio, like she's been with some of the other men. What Claudio brings out in her is a loose kind of calm; her shoulders soften, and she laughs more. Not as much as with Kaleb but more than when she's just with me. I wish I was enough to make her happy—that it could just be the two of us and that would feel better to her than anything else.

Lately, in the evenings she's been playing her guitar for us, and the music is so beautiful even the walls sigh and sway. Every time though, there is a shift when the air in the room stops moving and suddenly Mom says it's way past my bedtime.

Laying there in the dark of my closet, Moonshadow sits in the back corner on a pile of fresh alfalfa. His ears are down and resting as he blinks his beautiful black eyes, trying to tell me something I don't quite understand. I fall asleep listening to Mom and Claudio's laughter from the kitchen, then quiet movements—the scrape of a chair and the springs of the couch, and then finally the soft animal noises through my closet wall. Mom painted it a pale yellow last weekend to try to cheer things up. She brought home a packet of glow-in-the-dark stars too, for me to stick on the walls and the ceiling if I get a chair to stand on.

"You can make some constellations," she told me. "You can make a whole universe."

*It's been so cold and gray it feels like summer barely hap-*pened, but Mom gets me a packet of new pencils, lined paper, and a binder with a pouch to keep everything in. Mom is ready for school to start because she can't afford for me to be at the YMCA so much, and "When is this hamster wheel going to stop?" she mumbles, but I don't have any answers—I don't think she was talking to me anyway.

"Small body, big brain," she said on the first day, tapping her temple and smiling. She showed me how to walk to school on my own because it's not very far.

I told Moonshadow to make himself scarce without me there to protect him and reminded him he can always go to our closet if he doesn't want to be around Claudio. I left extra hay and water and petted him three times on his ears for luck. Mom and I walked up our road toward State Street, which is busy with no light. She said if I stand at the corner and wait with my book bag showing, people will eventually stop and then I can go. We got across State Street and then went down another street with more houses and fewer trees. I felt sorry for the people living there, with their bigger houses but no room outside for the deer and raccoons and fields of grasses. Down farther were some gray buildings and a short alleyway that took us to the school.

"Couldn't be easier, right? Especially since you've already

made it home from a bar alone at night." She shakes her head but seems a little bit proud of me, like I've got what it takes.

She gave me a hug and said to follow the breadcrumbs back the same way to get home, that she would leave the key under a rock next to the back steps to get in, and I should make myself a bowl of cereal if I get hungry—that she would be home by six-thirty to make a special dinner for her grown-up third-grader.

School started a week ago and the walk is no longer fun or inter-esting. Turns out, no one stops on State Street for kids, and I just have to wait until all the cars and trucks pass and then run across as fast as I can.

Behind the school and across a fenced-off lot is the can-nery where Mom once told me she worked when she was in high school, trying to save up money to enroll at Northwest Art Academy. She said it was always too cold or too hot there, depending on the season, and it was always women who worked the lines. In those women she saw what she didn't want for her-self—their bent backs, saggy skin, and sour faces looking sickly in the dim lighting. Some of the women who worked there had parts of their fingers missing from accidents with the belts and gears. Some, she said, had missing teeth, when they were too young to have lost their teeth. She said it's because America doesn't care about women or poor people. Mom wasn't even the youngest one working there. She had a younger friend named Maria who helped get her the job. A few years after Mom grad-uated from high school, Maria was murdered by her boyfriend at her parents' house on 21st Street when she was seventeen. She was pregnant and the baby inside her got murdered, too. Mom never made it to art school, but she's never told me why.

During lunch, Toby and I slip out from the side door and watch the gray steam rising up from the cannery. I haven't been able to eat today—my stomach teeth have been gnawing and chomping hard. I grabbed two cartons of milk from the crate when the lunch lady was yelling at Tyler not to push, yelling loud enough for the whole cafeteria to hear how he has to wait his turn the same as everyone else. I grab one chocolate, one plain, and can't decide which one will make my stomach teeth calm down the quickest.

Toby got teased a lot last year, and got treated badly even by the adults who were supposed to try and help. The grown-ups are not mean to him in obvious ways, they don't yell or anything; they do it in ways that are harder to catch. Ms. O'Brien never called on Toby, even when he used to want to answer the questions. This year, Mr. Kohl isn't any better.

Toby is different from the other boys—last year he drew ocean waves on his math sheets, wave after wave, looked out the window for too long, and refused to play dodgeball during recess. Now, Toby spends class with his head down, drawing hundreds of circles on the back of his subtraction worksheets instead, overlapping them in deeper and deeper pressings of his pencil, with jab-marks in the middle—so many poked-in eyeballs.

Mr. Kohl's classroom has a blue and green rug that is quickly turning brown. He keeps his Birkenstocks in a milk crate by his desk and teaches in thick wool socks, walking around the room in meandering circles. When he wears his black socks, his toe pokes out and looks like a hairy toad trying to escape. I mention it to Toby and he confirms men's toes often get gross and hairy. He makes a face and says he is definitely not going to let it happen to him.

We all get assigned jobs to do. Lola gets our free milk from the cafeteria and Brian is responsible for handing out our workbooks for math. Everyone laughs when I end up with the job of checking the fire alarm once a month, but when I get to climb up on a table to push the test button, everyone shuts up.

Mr. Kohl touches our backs when he walks by our desks and his hands are clammy and heavy—two cold steaks at the end of his thick arms. Ms. Julie is our student teacher this year. She has green eyes, and when she smiles, she has big dimples like someone you might see on TV. She wears tight, stretchy shirts that show how giant her breasts are, the largest ones I've ever seen by far. What's better than looking at them though is when she gives you a hug, and it's so soft and warm you never want her to let go.

Last week Ms. Julie was leaning over to say something in a low voice to Mr. Kohl but out of nowhere he got up and said he needed something in the copy room. His pants had gotten tighter in front, like his zipper might pop open. Toby said it's called a boner and lots of guys get it, but that Mr. Kohl shouldn't get one in class—that his mom explained that boners are something to be dealt with in the bathroom—but his dad said boners need to be stuck somewhere warm. "Then my parents started fighting again," he told me.

Ms. Julie has been helping out more in other classes for the past few days. She's getting away from Mr. Kohl's boner but she left us behind.

Kids are meaner to Toby than the adults. They call him a dicksucker and a poof and a fruitcake and make fun of the way he walks. He does walk kind of funny, up on his tippy toes—he's got extra air under his heels. In dodgeball, back when he used to try to play, he got reamed—an easy target—not ever able to catch the red ball as it pelted toward him at warp speed. Toby pretends he doesn't care but sometimes when he comes to sit with me, his nose is red and his eyes are rubbed raw because he's been off crying somewhere.

On the other side of the playground, kids scream and laugh, chase each other and yell about who has a crush on who. The girls are at the monkey bars swinging from their callused hands and talking about the boys, and the boys are throwing balls back and forth and talking about the cars they'll drive when they're older.

Toby keeps picking at a hole in his shoe and asks me if I've seen Foxy and her older stepbrother Edwin having sex in the alley down the road from our houses. What Foxy and Edwin do is not sex because they have their clothes on, but their bodies press together and move with a strange, unsettling rhythm while broken glass crunches under their sneakers and the wind blows trash over from I-5.

Foxy is a few years older than me, and Mom says to stay far away from her. Mom tells me Foxy's mom and stepfather have left her out for the wolves, and I am forbidden to go anywhere near their house—a sad, brown box surrounded by a large yard filled with dog crap and overgrown blackberry vines. Edwin is often out there, setting trash on fire, trying to do tricks in the driveway on his BMX bike, flipping people off if they catch him messing up. They have a dog named Bingo they keep tied up on the side. Bingo is skinny and alone and used to pull against his leash to play, but now all he does is sidestep his own shit within the half-circle of movement his chain allows him.

I imagine sneaking over to untie Bingo, and bringing him to our house where he would finally be warm and petted and fed all our best meat scraps, with no spiked collar and no short chain, and no Edwin. I can't save him though—I'm not big enough to stand up to Edwin and the rest of them. When I wake up late at night worried about Bingo out there all alone, cold in the silver moonlight, the teeth living in my stomach start growing longer and sharper—they are turning into horror movie butcher knives now, and they shine a hard silver.

"So you've seen Foxy and Edwin together?" Toby asks me again.

"Yeah, they do it against the wooden fence," I say.

I don't tell him that sometimes when I pass them, a needy ache blooms where my underwear rubs against my skin, and other times seeing them I am so worried and sick I have to go back to my closet to play solitaire, read, or make myself go to sleep just to put them out of my mind. I don't want to be Foxy and I'm not sure Foxy wants to be Foxy either.

"She's going to get a baby if they don't knock it off," Toby says, and I nod, but she's only eleven and I hope that's not how it works. Toby keeps going. "Edwin's got a huge dick for a kid. I've seen it pop out of his basketball shorts like a fat hot dog."

I haven't paid attention to Edwin's dick. I always keep my eyes on Foxy, studying her for a clue about something useful. I wonder if she likes what they do, or if she wants to be playing jacks on the sidewalk and riding bikes over broken concrete with the rest of us. She yelled *Hi* to me once from her yard, and I waved back, but maybe she didn't see me because now she won't look at me at all.

Behind the cannery smokestack, Toby starts picking at a scab on his elbow and watches the gray air rise, silent now. He hugs his knees to his chest and rocks back and forth, excited or upset or maybe both—sometimes it's hard to tell with Toby. He stares and rocks himself, maybe wondering about Edwin's big penis, maybe worried about some future baby or something worse. From his tight, sunken face it looks like he's thinking about a lot of terrible things, not only Foxy and Edwin but maybe his own problems, too—how there are so many things to worry about, coming down the line at us like the old cannery conveyor belt Mom described.

Toby doesn't know what I've watched going on at his house like a bad TV show, and I don't know how to ask him if he's okay. He might be embarrassed and get angry. Maybe if I ask he will get upset and leave me here alone.

A few nights ago, his dad was yelling at him so loudly all the dogs in our neighborhood started barking, and I went to the window to find out what was happening. I opened the curtain in time to see Toby shoved out the front door with his pants around his ankles. The push was so hard he lost his balance and fell off their porch into the cold mud below. He wasn't crying or anything, which made it even worse. He pulled up his pants crusted in mud, sat down on the front step, and pulled his knees tightly to his chest, rocking and rocking in the growing dark and waiting, like this had happened before and he knew how to handle it. I didn't know what to do and kept threatening to float up, trying to pretend nothing was wrong, that whatever was happening was no big deal.

Later he was still there, but not rocking anymore—sitting motionless in the dim blue of the porch light like a lonely old man. After dinner, while Mom was running me a bath, I pushed aside the curtains again—in time to see his mom open their front door a crack. She reached out her arms, which are even skinnier than Mom's, to lead him into their dark house like it was their special secret.

I line up my stuffed animals on the bed so they're leaning against my pillow, seated comfortably. I can't leave my closet until they are all there together, counted and safe. Snoopy, Raggedy Ann, and Sock Monkey. They have to be sitting close enough so part of each touches another—a hand or paw—so they know they're not alone.

Once I came home from school and Snoopy had fallen on the floor. I was sick to my stomach, thinking of him separated— cold and alone, not knowing when I'd come back to help him. I petted his head and put him back with the others, told them all I'd be more careful—I'd make sure it wouldn't happen again. And it hasn't.

I haven't done this in a while, but once I took off their clothes and looked between their legs where their mounds are. I was relieved to find nothing. I pulled down my pants and underwear and looked at myself, wishing I had a mound of nothingness, too—that nothing would ever go in and nothing would ever come out.

A lot of people say that when they first meet me they can't tell if I am a boy or a girl. Sometimes the not-knowing makes people look me up and down with confused looks on their faces, and when they can't figure it out some of them get angry. Some of them look at the door like they can't wait to leave, or straight-out ask Mom what I am—a question she never answers—she says they can go screw themselves all the way to hell if they are that concerned with the genitals of a child.

"If people just had mounds of nothingness, everything would be a lot easier," I say, but Mom has not been in a hearing kind of mood lately.

My name doesn't help with people's confusion. Mom is ready to tell me the story of it, as if it is no big deal and never was. She says she named me Smokey because that "Cruisin'" song by Smokey Robinson was on the radio constantly when she was pregnant. She never had cravings for chocolate milkshakes or cheese pizza, but she did crave those verses.

"The feeling I got listening to it was…" she drifts off, remembering, and looks for the album way in the very back of her crate full of records.

"Listen for yourself," she said as she put the song on the record player.

I understood what she meant and set the needle back to the

beginning so many times Mom said she thought I had gotten the idea and told me to put on something else.

Kids have always teased me about my name.

"Your mom must really love to smoke," they always snicker. I never admitted to them that I'd always wondered if that's why she named me Smokey, too.

Only Toby knows they should call me Rocky instead, but I don't even shadow box anymore—no more dancing around, light on my feet, dodging punches and faking lefts and rights. Sometimes though, I still punch my pillow when I get too mad.

So I am named after a smooth, soulful singer with perfect cheekbones and straight, gleaming teeth—not like all the snaggletooths who fill up Moss River Elementary School.

Mom and I are sitting on a bench downtown, eating day-old donuts we can get for five cents from the bakery there. She tells me she used to date Smokey Robinson's cousin up in Portland.

"I met Smokey once when I was pregnant with you, at a picnic. He and the guy I was dating could have been twins," she says, "so when he told me Smokey was his cousin, I completely believed him. I loved that name, so I gave it to you."

I stay quiet. I don't want to be named after some singer Mom met once, through some boyfriend Mom knew for no more than a few weeks. Besides, the name is too soft, too pretty. I want a tougher name, so people won't mess with me: *Rocky Washington.*

"When you date someone," she tells me, "it's important to try to get at least one great thing out of it. What I got from that one was a name for my future kid."

She presses the back of her hand against my forehead.

"You look feverish," she says, but I tell her I'm okay and keep nibbling at my donut, worried about taking big bites for what the teeth in my guts might do, wanting to make this sweetness last.

My stomach has been burning more lately, hot on the inside,

waking me up at night with sudden stabs, and this morning in the bathroom I checked before flushing and my poop was black with red in it. If I'm bleeding where my crap comes out, I'm worried it is probably something from what White Richard did. I want to forget that ever happened, but he keeps it up with his hauntings. No one can be told about White Richard because I might still get taken away.

"Let's go home and take your temperature," she says, and wipes some powdered sugar off my cheek with her finger—tells me to blow it off and make a wish.

Back at home with the thermometer under my tongue, she opens a faded envelope and shows me a photograph of when I was first born. I am fat and brown, with the head of thick black hair she'd described. At the bottom is the name Robinson.

"Why does it say Robinson on here if he wasn't my dad?" I ask her, folding the creases in the edges of the photograph, trying to put it together.

"At the last second, I thought I should be married when you were born, so I married Smokey Robinson's cousin. You don't need to know his name. We got it annulled a week later. It was all an awful mistake. Like I said, finding your name was the best part of the whole thing."

I imagine her still dating him, having stayed married to him even, and us both getting to gaze at those Robinson-family green eyes every day. But we don't have Smokey's cousin; instead, we have Claudio.

When there are no crops to pick, Claudio drinks beer. Sometimes he helps out around our house, fixing the fence or repairing a leaky faucet, but mostly he drinks. When I come home from school before Mom gets off work, there he is. We don't have much to say to each other—Mom is the bridge between us, and without her, we are nothing more than two people trying to avoid making eye contact in a small space.

"Where do you live when you're not here?" I asked him the last time we were alone together.

"With five pendejos in a trailer off Highway 99 in Freitas," he'd said, not making eye contact, and then went outside to his truck for no good reason. Sometimes he just sits there, fiddling with the radio with his rough, jumpy fingers.

Claudio's truck is red and drips oil in our driveway more and more often. It sits there leaking its guts out. From his rearview mirror hangs an air freshener—Jude the Apostle in faded neon. Sometimes when I come home from school, he is asleep on the couch, other times he's nervous and fidgety, walking around like he's done something wrong, but everything in the house seems normal. Lately, when I know he will be home in those hours before Mom gets off work, I stay at the school library or play games in the large, dusty field behind the mushroom processing factory with all the other kids who don't want to go home yet.

Today Claudio is passed out on the couch with the TV on. I walk by him on the way to my room, holding my breath and moving on tiptoes. Claudio is still and breathing in and out heavily. In his hand is his dick, huge and limp. I've taken Mom's *Joy of Sex* book off the shelf and thumbed through *Our Bodies, Ourselves,* but this is different. The air in the room is thick and musky. His nose hairs move in and out and I'm caught off guard when he opens his eyes to catch me staring at him. I expect him to be embarrassed with his dick hanging out, but he isn't. He looks at me with sleepy eyes and runs his hand over it as if he's petting a cat, finally pushing it down into his stretched-out, stained underwear and slowly zipping up his jeans. Then he closes his eyes with a strange calm, not bothered that I saw.

Back in my closet with the door closed and the flashlight on, my breath comes out in harsh gasps and the room spins, but I can hear him chuckling quietly to himself. Outside, the back gate clinks shut. I get up and go to the window in the hallway—there's David, our 22-year-old neighbor, looking behind him at our house and catching my eye. He waves at me but doesn't flash his usual, perfect, boy-smile.

At dinner, Mom senses my tenseness and asks me three times if I am alright, but I don't know what to say. I start floating off my chair, but hold on to it and focus on body weight, on bricks, on all my bones weighted down, heavy like Rocky Balboa. Claudio is going back for seconds and playfully slaps Mom on the butt with a dish towel, and with each sharp thwack, Mom's concern for me fades.

In the bathroom, only a little bit of blood is coming out, not as bad as before, but in the back of my throat I taste sharp metal. My stomach has puffed out into a sad, beige balloon and I suck it in so no one will worry I'm pregnant or that something else is wrong. White Richard's blurry ghost-head peeks around the corner and says he did this—he made it so I'd always feel this lonely quiet ache, this fear, this alien thing in my body. I still can't really remember what he looked like, but if I close my eyes, he grows taller—a large, pale shape glowing a sickly green and moving around like he's floating a couple of inches off the floorboards, riding through on his UFO.

Maybe, by now, the real White Richard—the one who has a real body and does normal, human things—has found himself another girlfriend to replace Mom. Maybe this new girlfriend he has leaves the house more often and doesn't know yet that she should always take her kids with her. Or maybe now he acts like a dad should; maybe these days he's feeling better and does his best not to hurt anyone.

Mom and Claudio are in the bedroom now and the animal moans crawl out from under the door frame like usual, only now I have a clear image of what the body parts are, and can see

Claudio's calm, sleepy face as Mom breathes fast and heavy through the walls.

My stomach teeth start jammering again, chomp chomping through all my fleshy insides, but there's no real escape here—our walls are too thin, even with pillows over my head, even with humming. Moonshadow is warm in his hay and doesn't mind the sounds, so I leave him there to get some rest—he's still a baby who needs his sleep. I get dressed, pull on my muddy boots, find my jacket, and follow the trail back to Old Oak.

The sounds are different out in the dark, and the smells are clearer, too. There's the pine sap smell, and the smell of the wet dirt, and there's the smell of smoke—maybe the people in the camp had a bonfire and told stories before laying their tired bodies down. When I get to Old Oak, she smells better than anything else, and I press the acorns that have fallen on the ground to my nose, inhaling their damp, clean scent.

Twigs snap behind me and then things get quiet, like someone is watching me. Maybe Claudio followed me out here and he's going to teach me a lesson about how bad I am, to tell me not to say anything about what I saw. But when I squint, there's no one there, and when I sniff the air, there's no one there. Claudio's cologne is a dead giveaway, and all I can smell is my tree. I keep an eye out until I can't focus anymore. My eyes are tired now and the night is complete.

I wake up, damp with the moisture from the ground, and unfurl my body from the tight ball I've curled myself into. The sun is coming up through the clouds above the field, covering everything in dull, orange light. I stand up and brush myself off, wrap my arms around Old Oak, and lean hard against her bark. I take the deepest breath of her I can and then start walking back toward our house, hoping Mom notices I was gone all night and is sorry.

Mom tells me about babies and periods when I ask for a little brother for Christmas. I think a little boy would be helpful here, imagine making him laugh, and how much happier he might make us.

"Never going to happen," Mom says and means it. "I'm barely making it by as it is. Aren't we enough, Smokes?"

We aren't enough.

Sometimes we are barely here at all, and the house is empty—heavy with stale air, and there is never any baby laughter, no unexpected shrieks of delight. Our laughter is more tired—it comes out, but just for a little bit, and then it wants to go back to sleep. Mom said she is on birth control so she doesn't get her period, and if she doesn't get her period, I'm not going to get a little brother.

"Period?" I'd asked, peeling back the skin from my fingernail, pulling it to the quick until it bled.

"When women reach a certain age, they start having a period once a month. It's on the same schedule as the moon and the tides, but everyone has theirs at a different time. Once a woman gets a period it means she could have a baby if she has sex."

"Do boys get periods?" I ask and Mom shakes her head no.

"Boys and men aren't tough enough for periods," she says. "They definitely couldn't handle it."

I don't know if I can handle it either, but I think about what I might do with my blood if the moon thing happens to me. I could smear it on my body in patterns like fingerpaint, could pour it down the front of my face so it looks like I was stabbed for Halloween. I imagine jumping out from behind a bush to scare Toby. I could really freak someone out.

I stand with my clothes off in front of the fake-gold framed mirror that Mom got at the Salvation Army thrift store. Mom says she doesn't like going there because they make the homeless people hear a church sermon before they're allowed to eat the free food.

"Not actually free, is it then?" she said that day, but it wasn't a question to answer. I am alone before the mirror with my clothes next to me in a pile. I examine myself.

Armpits. Nipples. Butt.

Everything on me is Moss River pale except a dark birth-mark, shaped like a tree leaf on the back of my calf. That is the color my whole body might have been, without all the German stock. My dark hair falls in curls over my forehead, my collar-bones are poking out and casting shadows downward from the overhead light.

Elbows. Wide nose. Ribs.

I turn around and spread my butt cheeks to look again at exactly where the poop comes out, then turn around in front to try to find my pee-hole.

Knees. Ears. Little teeth.

I open my mouth and look inside, move my tongue around and make sounds, watch my throat change shape. My voice lives down that hole, I think, and wonder what it looks like, that little person inside me who makes all my sounds—

Ooooooooooh, ahhhhhhhhhhhhh. Ooooooooooooh, ahhhhhhhhhhhhh.

It's Saturday and Mom is leaving to pick up some groceries.
She says she needs some alone time but that I can watch cartoons as long as I want, and there are frozen waffles to toast if I get hungry. Moonshadow sits next to me on the couch. I turn on the TV to watch cartoons but they're not funny like they used to be, nothing even makes sense. Bugs Bunny never gets tired—doesn't sleep, doesn't understand how to be quiet and still, and everything is just one big joke. I pick up Moonshadow and take him outside to his pen in the yard. He stretches out his legs, hops around, and chews a blade of grass like a real bunny should. We haven't had a clear day in a long time. I leave him there in the cool sun and make my way back to Old Oak, sit on the ground with my back against her bark, and keep an eye out for Deer.

If I don't move at all, fat beetles—their backs shiny with blackness—crawl over my jeans and up my hands to my arms. I'm the giant and I'm in their way. Mom says the smallest of animals have as much of a right to live their lives as we do. She avoids swatting flies, lets spiders live out their whole lives in the corners of our living room, and sometimes leaves honey for the ants outside.

No matter what I do or where I go, there is Claudio's dick in my mind—how it sat there, a tired pet ferret peeking out of his Levi's. Thinking of it makes me want to stick my finger down my throat, way deep down, to force myself to throw up this feeling. I'm hungry but won't ever be able to eat again until I make this boiling lava come out. I haven't seen Claudio's dick since that last afternoon, but even when he has his jeans on, it's there, sleepily pointing in my direction or away, asking Claudio to let him out. White Richard in his ghost-body keeps visiting, too, late at night in my closet when I can't sleep. I have to stay alert for signs of either of them and be ready to protect myself—to fight back like the real Rocky Balboa next time.

I pick the beetles off one by one to help them on their way, turn over to lay face down on the ground, and put my tongue to the dirt to taste. The clay dissolves, grit in my teeth, but I swallow anyway, and the sickness in my stomach lets up; the dirt is holding down the sour thing beneath. I eat some more, picking around the pebbles and stones to get to the soft stuff, bits of decaying oak leaf, the tiniest twigs, and the dark brown earth, still wet from all the rain we've been having.

The more dirt I eat, the heavier I grow—not like eating too much, but like I'm getting stronger. Maybe this simple thing will make everything better. I'll forget about Claudio's dick and I'll forget about White Richard. I rub my stomach three times for good luck and wipe the dirt from around my lips over and over to make sure it's clean. Mom wouldn't understand this. I brush myself off and head back to the house, finally full.

At school, the teachers hold an assembly to remind us to be careful near the river, because a younger boy named Noah Tucker, in Ms. Ruiz's kindergarten class, had an accident. His family went out on a raft during a break in the rain, when the sun cut through the clouds for a couple of hours. They were fishing over in West Moss River, across the bridge. Their narrow boat turned over quickly, and all of them went under. Within seconds everyone resurfaced except Noah, who had turned five the week before.

Now all everyone talks about is the missing body of that boy. On the five o'clock news, blue-suited men show his picture, have an interview with his family. If Noah was somehow found alive and had a chance to grow up, he would look a lot like David. Mom comes to look at the TV and Claudio comes with her.

"Doesn't he look like a kid version of David?" I ask them.

Claudio lets a strange look move across his face, and Mom says, "Sure, kinda. I get what you mean," but she is distracted and wants to get back to making vegetable soup.

Discounted swim classes are being offered at the community center and altars have been set up along the river's shores, with water safety warnings broadcast on the news every night at five. After school, some of the older kids ride their bikes along the river, hoping to be the ones to find Noah's body.

At night I keep having the same thought over and over. It's

the idea of a body not floating back up, and how it must feel underneath all that dirty wetness. The river floods my dreams. It's a heavy blanket I can't find the way out from underneath. It holds me down until I get too tired, can't open my eyes, and fall asleep again beneath it.

David honks his horn on accident and wakes Moonshadow and me up. It is morning, but the sun hasn't risen above the tree line yet. David is always around because he never left home for college or anywhere else and lives on the other side of Toby's house, in a mobile home with his dad. He works on cars in their driveway for cash, and Mom has hired him a few times for help with the Volkswagen, whose sputters keep getting louder. I still think about the gas station boy, and even for a quick errand, a sick churning burns when I climb into the passenger seat. I want a different car, but Mom says we have to keep the one we have running for as long as we can.

David still looks like a teenager, with a cuteness about him that prevents anyone from treating him like a grown man. That's what Mom says. He is still a boy with no facial hair, usually wearing his fading high school varsity jacket.

Mom found them together yesterday. There was an electrical fire at the warehouse and her boss sent all the workers home early. I was still at school. She wasn't surprised to find Claudio's truck in the driveway, but when she walked up the front steps, she stood there looking through the living room window from the outside as the minutes ticked by. She said it took time standing there to understand what was happening.

She told me the details when I got home, that Claudio and David were having sex on the couch.

"I need you to have the whole truth so you can avoid making my same mistakes," she said.

I have questions, but not about mistakes—about this sex between men and how it works, and isn't Claudio too old for David? I keep these questions to myself because Mom won't want to answer them—maybe she can't.

I'm still fighting to erase the image of Claudio's dick, worry I'm stuck with it forever, just like I'm stuck with the gas station boy, like I'm stuck with White Richard. Here is Claudio's dick in my mind now, less like a ferret and more like a scraggly Russet potato past its prime. Mom expects me to be more surprised than I am when she's done telling me everything, but it is all too easy to picture: football on the TV, sweat stains spreading. I still don't tell her that I've already seen Claudio's dick, that something's been off for a while. David's dick probably isn't as gross as Claudio's wrinkled potato, and even though Mom is upset and nothing makes any sense, a warm pulsing starts between my legs—a strange ache that I don't want to end. I pick up Moonshadow from the kitchen where he's eating carrot scraps and sit on the couch while Mom cries into her hands, her shoulders heaving in the growing darkness.

I love the calm, clean feeling when a boyfriend gets kicked out, and even though Mom is sad, it's better that Claudio is gone, gone, gone forever. The only proof he's ever been here are Mom's tears and a thick trail of black oil that spots the driveway. The house barely smells of yeast or Old Spice anymore—Mom's been scrubbing the couch with steaming hot water and a strong detergent that makes her knuckles pink and angry.

On the ten o'clock news, the reporters say that they found Noah Tucker's body over by the old Boise Mill. Mom's back tenses as it moves with the effort of cleaning. She won't stop scrubbing—this motion is the only thing still keeping her here and alive and in a body. It's the only thing that matters to her right now. The detergent is strong medicine, but the loneliness birds keep flying in slow circles over her head.

She unbends herself finally, turns around, and looks at me carefully—with more focus than she has in a while, then moves closer to hug me.

"We're finally going to get a new car," she tells me. "David's not going to be working on our old one anymore."

I flash from Noah to David, to the car, to the boy at the gas station, flames around his skinny shoulders.

"Smokey, you know I love you, right?"

I nod. I understand her messy, painful love and the way I need it and sometimes get it and sometimes don't. It's in the way she looks at me when she's calm, and the way she washes my back with a warm washcloth in the bath sometimes. It's in the way she leaves me colorful notes in my pockets, telling me I'm smart and strong and that she loves my almond-shaped eyes that notice everything.

"Will you put the song on for us?" she asks.

I cross the living room, past her bucket of hot water, and put the needle down on the record. My namesake's perfect voice fills the air, more solid and clear than anything.

In the darkness of my closet, I can make the warm feelings come, and I know this is something about why Mom needs men, and also about periods and babies and sex. I do it even though I could get pregnant. I know enough to know getting pregnant from this is something that could go into the Guinness Book of World Records, but still, it might happen to me because I'm not like other people—there's something different about me.

My hands move without any effort.

Armpit. Ribs.

Hip. Stomach.

Neck. Hair.

Foot. Calf.

Knee. Thigh.

There. There.

This is the medicine for making everything else disappear. It brings the animal thinking and the animal breathing and the animal skin. It brings heaviness and lightness and need and quiet. I turn into a coyote and the hair on my arms grows coarse. Everything is alive, I have to remember that. We are all just animals under our two-legged walking. This is what we can remember when we lie down like they do. I am catching my breath and remembering who I really am.

—

Mom opened the door the last time I became an animal, the bright light hurting my eyes because I had adjusted to the other place. She asked me what I was doing in there in the dark.

"Practicing," I said, without thinking, and then showed her my teeth and growled.

"Okay," she said, trying not to laugh but also giving me a strange look, like she'd never be able to figure me out. "I'll make you some hot chocolate. Come out of there and have some."

She left the door wide open as she walked away, and I knew I would have to be more careful from now on because I was learning this new way to be that was only for me.

Toby's mom has red hair and green eyes that look hollowed out. She wears yellow sandals that show her toes have chipped nail polish and are dirty. Mom tells me that during the Spanish Inquisition, red-haired women were thought to be witches who had stolen hell's fire. Toby says his mom only sometimes steals makeup from Matthiesen's. She is the kind of skinny like she hasn't eaten in weeks, and her skin is so pale that if you got close enough and reached out your finger, you could trace the blue veins under her wrists and arms, all the way up her neck. I haven't gotten close to Toby's mom very often, but once she offered me a box of animal crackers and that's when I saw her veins. Toby calls her by her first name, Cherry. Mom would not like to be called anything except Mom, but Cherry doesn't seem to mind.

Cherry is always rushing around like she drank too much coffee, which Mom calls *the jitters*, and now she's got a new boyfriend, too. Toby never ended up stabbing his dad but got him to leave anyway—or maybe Cherry did, and Toby is taking all the credit.

Toby's dad lives in Tucson, Arizona now, and sent Toby a t-shirt with a cactus on it. Toby says his dad can go to hell and that he's going to throw the t-shirt in the garbage, but he probably won't.

Toby tells me his mom's new boyfriend's name is Hank. Out

of earshot, we call him Hanky-Panky and can't stop laughing. Toby looks over at me and says we should become blood brothers, and he'll get the stuff we need to make it official. Later in the afternoon, I watch Toby and Hanky-Panky unloading groceries across the road. Hanky is a slouchy weasel, with close-set eyes and a pointy chin.

Once they go inside, I find Mom in the kitchen and ask her why she doesn't bring white men home.

"Well, I did once," she says.

White Richard.

She takes a deep breath and looks around the room for her Lucky Strikes, but I've started hiding them in places where it will take her a while to find them—an Easter egg hunt for Mom that she doesn't know about or want to be playing. Mr. Kohl says smoking turns your lungs black and showed us pictures from a magazine that we passed around the room in science class. Toby made a gagging sound as he looked between the healthy lungs and smoking lungs, while I seared the pictures into my mind and started making my plan.

"White men can't be trusted. I don't know why exactly, but they just can't."

The first white man in her life was her father, Jack—a tall, stiff-looking man who always wore a freshly pressed suit and killed himself before I was born. She only has a couple pictures of him. Mom mostly tries to pretend he didn't exist and won't answer questions about him. I found out as much as I have from listening when she was talking to Angela on the phone once.

She looks out the window, probably thinking about all the men she has known, and I want to point out to her that all but one have been awful—not just that one extra-terrible white one. I try to remember how Kaleb smelled, but can't bring it back anymore. He's too far gone now, and more and more lately, Mom disappears just like her Lucky Strike smoke, unless she is the one bringing up the horrible things. She's figured out my trick of floating up.

I make a list in my mind of all the white men from the TV shows I watch—Charles from *Little House on the Prairie*; Gilligan stranded on his island; Mike from *The Brady Bunch*; the captain of *The Love Boat*; and Jack on *Three's Company*. I can't imagine Mom falling for any of them, but if she asked, I would be up for giving one of them a chance at least. The Cat Stevens record with the orange cat on it leans against our bookshelf. Cat Stevens would make a great boyfriend for Mom, but I don't know how I could get him to come to Moss River. I can't imagine he would want to, not for us.

Toby's stories about Hanky-Panky are all bad.

"He calls me 'Shit-for-Brains,' and his underwear are always dirty. He doesn't wash his hands after taking one of his big, gross shits—nasty! He carves naked women with big titties out of hunks of wood. His breath smells like rotten meat. He breaks things for no reason. We never know what he's going to do next."

Toby says no-big-deal things set Hanky-Panky off, like if Toby doesn't make his bed or set the table right, even though Hanky-Panky never lifts a finger to clean or make the house better.

"Also," Toby tells me, "his dick is very, very small, kind of like a little carrot."

We both laugh but my teeth-knives start up. *How does Toby know that?*

"I don't want you going over to Toby's anymore, ever," Mom says tonight. "He can come over here when I'm home or you two can play in the fields before it gets dark, but I don't want you over there. It's not safe."

I ask if I can still get a ride with Toby to school sometimes when it's raining extra hard, and she tells me no, because Hank is a psychopath and I should never get in a car with him.

"But Cherry takes him to school," I say, and she repeats that she doesn't want to take any chances, and besides, walking is great exercise and will help me grow up healthy and strong. Especially if it's raining.

"You won't have to take so many baths," she says, "Nature will clean you."

Her jaw is set hard. She's not going to change her mind on this one, and I haven't even told her anything about the things Toby said about Hanky-Panky—maybe she has watched them through the curtains, too—or maybe she just knows.

Mom is still single and makes special salads for Moon-shadow, asks me more questions, and reads her books by Collette. She never reads when there's a boyfriend, but now she sits on our couch by the window most nights and sips tea or wine and turns the pages slowly.

I watch Mom from across the room, moving back and forth in a rocking chair she found on sale at Goodwill. It's missing one arm, but the wood is warm brown and the motion she makes feels like a lullaby. She looks up from her book, her whole face a question.

"Do you ever think about what happened with Richard when you were younger? Do you ever remember anything?"

I look up at the ceiling and try not to go up there, then down at the floor. *Keep me down here, keep me down here*, I say to it. The teeth in my stomach start grinding, but they're not chomping yet. They're waking up from a short nap and aren't quite ready for a fight.

"I don't remember anything," I tell her, "only what you told me."

"I had something similar happen to me once, when I was still a kid, but a lot older than you."

For Mom, it was a doctor her mother had taken her to when she was having painful cramps from her period. She said she knew there was something off about the doctor right away, but she didn't trust her instincts. He said some cramping was normal but there were things he could do to make it hurt less.

"He had me lie down and pressed on my stomach and my hips, massaged my legs, and then rubbed my breasts, which didn't make any sense—I knew it was wrong. And then right when I thought it was over, he put his finger inside and poked around, and his face got red, and he made sounds that scared me. I didn't know what those sounds meant then, but I do now. I wanted to scream and fight him and yell, but I didn't. I thought my mother would be embarrassed because it would turn out that what he was doing was completely normal and I'd made a huge deal out of nothing, which everyone said I always did anyways."

She looks out the window and takes a deep breath. The curtains flap in the draft. Even though it's stormy outside, Mom has been keeping the windows open. The house still smells of the detergent she used on the couch, and there's also something underneath that smell—she wants this storm to help air it all out for good.

"I'm telling you this because it's of the utmost importance that you trust your gut," she says, making a fist and placing it right below her rib cage. "In here," she says. "I'm also telling you this so you understand that even though a bad thing happened to me, and a bad thing happened to you, we can still have happy lives that don't have anything to do with the bad thing. Probably other bad things will happen, because that's just what life is like, but I'll still be okay and you'll still be okay."

She wants to say more, but instead takes a long drag on her cigarette, closes her Collette book, and sets it on the side table.

"This probably won't make sense to you, at least not yet, but for a long time I thought all I had to offer was a body. You need to understand that you have a lot more to offer than that."

"Is this why you always want a boyfriend, why it can't be the two of us?"

She puts out her Lucky Strike by dipping the burning tip in a glass of water. It sizzles as she turns to face me.

"Yes. I need another grown-up sometimes, Smokes, even though I often wish I didn't."

She motions for me to come over. I sit on her lap and rest my head in the crook of her neck, and she wraps her arms around me. Outside, it starts raining harder, the sound of the raindrops on our roof creating a steady pounding that matches her heartbeat thumping hard against her rib cage.

Moonshadow hops in from the other room, sniffing around and dragging a piece of hay behind him. He sits back on his hind legs and cleans his ears, eyeing us like this is his house and we are the visitors. *You're both so calm today*, he says. *Let's do this more often.*

When I grow up, I will have a house full of animals and won't need any humans. I'll make breakfast and dinner for them and make sure everyone is enjoying themselves and healthy and, that no one grows any stomach teeth.

My house will be a small camping tent like the one in the ad on the back of *Boys' Life* magazine, with a field and trees and open sky all around for hawks and eagles. The animals won't have to worry about getting run over or pelted with rocks or shot with a BB gun because there won't be any humans for miles around. I won't even be a human anymore, I'll have started turning into a deer by then, with larger eyes and more sensitive ears and antlers that I need to scratch on trees. Most nights I won't even go inside the tent to sleep; I'll lay in the soft grass I've made into a bed and listen to the nightbirds and watch the stars until my eyes are too heavy to keep open.

Mom starts laughing and teases, "Where did you go? You were a million miles away."

I tell her that when I grow up I might be a deer and only live with the animals, and she says that sounds wonderful and she hopes I will let her visit sometimes.

She gets up to fix dinner for us, chicken and mashed potatoes, my favorite. Outside, the rain keeps coming, and there are deepening ruts in the road along the curb, with leaf-boats floating by. The sky is dark purple with no stars out, only clouds and darkness and quiet. I hope Deer is safe with her mother, hope the owls are safe, too.

"I guess winter came early," Mom says from the kitchen, though it feels like winter has been here the whole time, that it never really leaves us in Moss River.

I pick up Moonshadow and hum his name-song under my breath while the onions simmer to golden brown on the stove. My guts tell me that for now we are loved and protected, and my stomach teeth are the quietest they've been in a long time.

Toby says David is moving out, says he's going to New York
City. Toby wants to go with him because David says there are
places not even that far away that aren't so wet. David says there
are places where heat is the problem. And there are places where
there are fewer bigots and so many different kinds of people that
the world feels a lot bigger, and where you could get lost but
also where you could get found. I don't believe David wants to
take Toby along, but Toby seems to think it's a real possibility.
He even packed a bag in case it's a short-notice kind of thing.
I wonder if Toby knows he's more than just a body, but I don't
know how to ask him. While he talks about seeing the Grand
Canyon and Niagara Falls with David, and how they'll be like
blood brothers but even closer than that, I watch a row of ants
make their way in a long line between our feet, living their whole
lives while we live ours—their tiny bodies every bit as vibrant,
building whole kingdoms out of nothing.

Mom comes home with an easel and a white canvas stretched tight over wood. She goes into the basement to bring out old paints from a dusty, wooden box I've never seen before. The paint tubes are crusty, but Mom says they can still be used if enough turpentine is added. The colors are too vivid until she mixes them, making subtle shades, and she tells me to get the folding chair because we are going to the back field, and she's going to paint my portrait.

"I've been wanting to do this for a long time," she tells me, looking at my face with steady, unhurried eyes.

As we walk out along the deer trail, slippery with mud, she tells me she tried to paint my portrait once when I was a baby, but even though she kept trying different angles, different paints, and different canvases, she could never get it to turn out.

"You just looked like a little blob," she says. "Now, though, you're starting to look like a real person."

She carries all her painting supplies, rags, and a hot thermos of coffee. I carry the folding chair, a bag of crackers, and an illustrated book that teaches the different kinds of clouds. I don't want Mom to notice something here in this patch of wildness where I spend my time alone, hiding from her and the things she does, the sounds she makes—worry something will be revealed that I want to keep private. Maybe beneath Old Oak, she'll be able to tell where my tongue tasted the clay dirt, or where Toby sits when he's quiet and doesn't want to talk but doesn't want to go home either. But Mom doesn't ask any questions. She watches the grasses sway and listens to the sounds from the camp. A thin figure in the distance is doing dishes and clanking metal pots, and someone yells while a motor starts up and revs in a low growl.

"I want you to sit under this tree, with your back to the camp, facing me," she says, and helps me set up my chair on a level patch of earth.

Sitting there, my view is of Mom, the trail leading back to our house, and Old Oak's branches—her long limbs reaching out in all different directions, extending her bare arms out toward us. The bones of Mom's wrists poke out—her own living, breathing skeleton. Mom tells me my skin catches the light and shadows perfectly. I am hungry for this close attention but also want to hide—put a blanket over my head, or at least be turned at an angle slightly away from her bright stare. I wish Deer would come out from behind the blackberry bushes, walk over to where I sit and lay her head in my lap. Mom would be speechless and still, staring at me like I am the most special person in the world, and I imagine how proud she would feel, having a kid who could make friends with wild animals. The heaviness of Deer's tawny head would keep me here, secure under the weight of her beauty, and all the other feelings would fade away.

Mom smiles at me, mixes her paints, and pours her coffee from the thermos into the little red cup attached to the top. The steam rises and disappears just like the smoke from her Lucky Strikes does. I wonder if she's been a witch all along without me knowing it, and evaporating the things she loves is her most practiced spell.

She hums a song I haven't heard before, and she is not heavy and tired; she is full of light, like she's been lifted up out of all her struggles and worries, and now is holding herself up here before me, full of her own brilliance. She's a crow today, her body so industrious—her old, black coat pulled tight around her shoulders. It would be completely natural if she started picking up acorns and cracking them open with her beak.

Mom says I can move my head around for now if needed, but to keep my body still. I look up at the clouds and check their shapes and patterns in my book. These low clouds could mean rain soon, but Mom isn't worried. She mixes her paints and dabs at the canvas, tilts her head, and squints to observe me better.

"How come even though you saved money at the cannery you didn't go to art school?" I ask her, and she winces and sighs.

She doesn't say anything—dabs one of the longer brushes in the brownest of the paints and looks up at the trees then back at me.

"Someone I thought knew better than me said I didn't have what it takes. So I quit."

Her old paintings that are tucked away in the basement could be in museums. She told me still-life sketches were her favorite, trying to capture ordinary beauty—a kitchen table with flowers starting to wilt, a blue bowl filled with oranges, a notebook on an old desk with a photograph of a young child off to the side, staring out but not smiling.

She keeps dabbing and painting, taking deep breaths between sips of coffee from the thermos.

"Who told you that you wouldn't make it?" I ask, wanting to find them, kick them, punch their stomach in like the real Rocky would—to show them they made a terrible mistake.

"It was my father who told me, your Grandfather Jack," she says. I look down at my hands because I can't do anything about that—he's been dead for a long time.

"He didn't believe in anyone but himself," she continues. "He was the hardest on me because I was sensitive, like you. He was also sensitive but hated that part of himself. He probably could have been a great artist, honestly, but he was an accountant and bitter because of it. I'm glad you never had to be around him."

With her voice so sad and her brown hair falling around her shoulders, I think she's going to give up and put everything away, but when I start to move she says to sit still and not to look down at my hands or at the book anymore, to stare right at her.

My stomach clenches and loosens and tightens into a fist. The teeth-knives are starting up again even though nothing's wrong. Then I see them coming for her from behind—a long line of angry men, small and furious in their accountants' suits, led by Grandfather Jack. I want to yell at them to go away, to not come any closer, but Mom warned me to sit still, and I can only hope they disappear before their footfalls become any more real.

Mom says she sometimes wishes her dad was still here, that maybe if he had been able to grow older, he would have let himself have more pleasure—to follow his instincts and not have to do only what was expected. She tells me this is one of the great burdens on men, that they are taught to be only one way, and how it poisons them and everything they touch. Mom says she misses her father even though his love was painful—it wasn't all his fault, but then says again it's better he didn't live long enough to damage me, too.

"Sometimes not having a father is better than having one," she says, but I don't know how it's better to have these other men either—these hungry visitors, these White Richards and Claudios and even Kalebs, coming to us with their anger or sadness or pain in one way or another, and then leaving whether we want them to or not.

This is the longest we've gone without a man, and the days stretch out longer now. They're quieter and calmer, and each morning it is possible that the day could be easy, with no stomach teeth and no stomach knives, and no broken dishes or broken doors or broken hearts.

Men take up a lot of time, and now that it's just us we have a lot more of it to spare.

Mom's been making homemade bread lately, the smell of each rounded loaf filling up the house in a way that makes my stomach go completely still, like we are in a warm cloud and nothing can hurt us. She read almost all the Collette books and has moved on to others, studies birds and color theory, and takes long baths. She keeps me off the TV, and we play games while the records spin on the record player: Old Maid, Crazy 8's, and Gin Rummy. I haven't played Solitaire in weeks. We eat dinner with our shoulders relaxed and sometimes remember to go look at the stars if the clouds decide to part. I don't have to abruptly go to bed now either. My bedtime is eight p.m. every night, and once I've crawled into my closet, Mom comes in to bring me water or to rub my back while I fall asleep, and I can feel that she doesn't want or need to be anywhere else.

Above us, Old Oak's branches creak against each other. The wind is picking up.

"We'll have to bring Moonshadow next time," she says. "It wouldn't be right to paint your portrait and not have him on your lap."

She shows me what she's done so far, the chair I'm sitting on and most of my body, still headless, with the greens and browns of the field behind me, the cloud book tucked under my arm.

"Maybe you could put a deer in, too," I say, and she smiles.

"That's a great idea, Smokes," she says and means it.

When I start getting too cold from not moving and can't sit still very well, Mom says we should take a break. She wipes the paint off her hands on the thighs of her old pants, sips the last of her coffee, and squints into the distance, but I can't tell what she sees—all is quiet at the camp now. She tells me to do five jumping jacks to warm up and comes over to button my jacket all the way up and pull the hat down over my ears.

"You spend time here, don't you?" she asks, but nothing is out of place that could have given me away. I look around for clues as to how she knows. "It's okay, Smokes, I'm glad you have this place. Everyone should have a quiet, peaceful place to go."

"Where's your peaceful place?" I ask her, and she says she always thought her peaceful place would be with another person—that it wouldn't matter where they were, just being together would be enough—they could be poor and hungry and sitting on a rotting porch, but it would all be just right. She says I'm lucky to have found a place I love already—that maybe I don't need people as much as she does or in the same way.

"You just need your animal friends and your trees, and I hope it's always like that for you. I hope that's always enough."

I wonder how she knows these things. I wonder what else she notices but doesn't talk about. I want to tell her that maybe I'm her special person, but I know she means it's a man she needs. I try to picture Mom at her happiest, but can't picture a person or place that would make it so. Even when she's painting and seems so alive, I can watch as all the terrible memories flutter around her like brown moths, rest on her shoulders and weigh her down.

"I got you a present," she says, "because I think you might be an artist like me." She steps over to her bag, hunches over, rummaging. She pulls out a black book and a silver pen. "There were more colorful ones, but I thought you might like black. You're serious like that."

She smiles and hands it to me and I feel the thick cover, the cool of the metal pen.

"It's a journal," she says, "for you to write down your ideas and stories and thoughts."

Like yours, I almost say, but stop myself.

I open the thick, inky cover and flip through the inside pages, blank and new.

"I chose this one because it doesn't have any lines, so you can also use it to sketch, to draw. If you want. Do you like it?"

I keep moving my fingers across the thick, soft pages, look up at her and ask what I should write about first.

"My advice," she tells me, leaning over to hold me by the shoulders so she can look right into my eyes, "is to write about the things you feel and notice and want."

Feel and notice and want.

A clap of thunder sounds in the distance and rain starts coming down. The air turns colder, but sweeter, too, and the softened dirt beneath our feet starts to go slick. We scramble to fold up the chair and the easel, turn the painted side of the canvas down so the rain won't mess up Mom's work. I tuck my new journal into the back of my pants. She takes off her black coat and lays it over the painting. She doesn't look like a crow anymore—now she's just a regular person trying to not let this one thing be ruined.

We make it back to the house as the rain turns from a steady drizzle to heavy drops beating down. She helps me out of my wet clothes and wraps a towel around me, drying off my hair and warming me up.

"I wanted to tell you that I've met someone new," she says.

The calm, easy feelings that have been building crumble out of me, littering the floor with dust, and my stomach teeth start grinding around—they've had time to rest and now are ready to finish the job—figuring out what to eat next.

"He's different from the others, and you'll like him. He wants to meet you, too. I told him all about you."

Mom says she loves me and she's going to make us some hot tea with honey, for me to sit by the heater and warm up. I pick up the canvas and lean it against the wall, sit down, and look at my reflection. There I am in my field, surrounded by the greens and browns, all alone—no Moonshadow and no Deer and no Old Oak. They're not in the painting, but the shadows casting off Mom are almost reaching my headless body, alone forever, with my arms frozen at my sides, like I'll never move again.

Under the fig tree, three slugs make their way across a muddy expanse. I'm outside in bare feet, letting the wet dirt push up between my toes, each step a sucking sound. I squat down low to watch them—brown bodies with ovals of dark—leaving their trails. I put my face next to theirs, hold my breath. They stop moving, but their antennas are working hard. Mr. Kohl read us a book chapter about how a slug's antennas are actually its eyes. That they don't see the same way we do, but they can see the light in ways we can't.

I back up to let them go on their way, making sure I am not blocking their ability to see. I close my eyes and try to let my antennas come out, to try to understand the brightness as well as they do, but heavy clouds have come over us now, and everything is a shadow.

The rain comes down in sheets of silver, and the wind blows from the west. The trees lean toward us, listening in. Right when we woke up, all the lights went out in a poof, and the refrigerator stopped humming. Mom gets out candles in case we still need them later, puts on water for tea, and lights some incense. Mom loves a storm, especially on a Saturday morning when there's nowhere to go.

I haven't met her new boyfriend—I imagine him coming over with a gleaming belt buckle, demanding to be fed, pounding on the walls and yelling about his problems. Then I try to picture someone like Kaleb, someone quieter who pays attention to things and offers to set the table, fold napkins. Whoever he is, it is possible she already got rid of him, because she's not saying anything—though she did go out last night after she thought I was asleep. I heard the door double-lock and the sound of the car roaring to life. We never got rid of our old Volkswagen but it hasn't broken down lately—it understands there's no one to fix it anymore. Falling back asleep is easier with Moonshadow for company. And unless something happens, Mom won't stay away for too long. I asked her if she visits her new boyfriend at night and she said no, she can't visit him at night, that it's not allowed. I imagine her out driving alone in the dark, listening for the night herons. She doesn't want to tell me where she goes but I know the most important part—she goes away from me.

This morning she's wearing her wrinkled clothes from yesterday, her hair a bird's nest in the back. She's bitten down her nails and now they're pink with dried blood around the edges. She sees me looking and sets her slender hands down in her lap to rest while the wind helps the trees scratch the roof.

"What's the first thing you remember?" she asks.

I remember leather shoe laces and learning to tie them, I remember oranges poked with cloves simmering on the stove in water, I remember a stray cat, white but dirty, that Mom tried to nurse back to health, I remember the crows that sat on the branches of the dead tree all winter, I remember the smell of daphne blooming in February, I remember feeding the ducks in Mill Creek, I remember a yellow raincoat, I remember an ice storm and icicles like daggers, I remember blood on the yellow linoleum floor, I remember drinking from the hose, I remember Mom slamming cupboards and swearing, I remember her war cry: goddamnsonofamotherfuckingbitch. I remember the smell of the new books in the library, I remember how big the big kids were, I remember the ramp to the kindergarten classroom, I remember show-and-tell and not bringing anything, I remember pulling out a tooth too soon and the tearing feel of it, I remember baths with Mom back when she would still get in with me, warm, I remember being even smaller and how impossible that seems already.

But those aren't the first things. I look at her pale lips and her pale eyes. I go back as far as I can.

"I remember nursing from your breast," I say and look away, but Mom doesn't get weird about body parts, "That's the very first thing."

She taught me to say breasts, not boobs, and the difference between labia and the vagina, too, and that dicks and cocks are nothing more than penises. Mom taught me these things after she picked me up from the YMCA and I told her I'd heard some boys talking about cunts in the hallway.

"If anyone uses the word cunt around you, get away from them as fast as you can," she'd instructed me.

Those boys had red sores on their faces and wallet chains clanking against their hips, their lanky bodies cloaked in heavy mean-boy smells—motor oil and sweat and frustration.

Mom nods at my nursing memory and says I have a strong mind, like an elephant.

"And I also remember that bottle shaped like a bear and how you always warmed the milk up for me."

I remember the bear's smile and that he was wearing blue overalls, and how the milk always made my insides warm.

"I was upset when you got rid of that bottle," I tell her, missing it now more than ever. Maybe if she had kept it, my stomach wouldn't hurt so much. I could hide it at school to help me with my stomach knives.

"Yeah," she says about the bottle. "I'm sorry for getting rid of it, but I thought it was time. And I have a problem with getting rid of things too soon."

She smiles a sad smile, and she is not thinking of the bottle but of bigger things, men and others, maybe me, too. Maybe we will all be gotten rid of when the time is right.

"How about you?" I ask her. "What's your first memory?"

"I remember being so young I couldn't talk yet, and I was being taken care of by my Aunt Josephine—you never met her—my father's younger sister. She had always made everyone in the family nervous but even more so after she found a Ouija board at an estate sale when she was around thirteen. She started doing seances with her friends in the tool shed when all the other kids from her school were at the Saturday night dances downtown. She wore old-timey dresses made of heavy black lace and let her hair grow wild and tangled. People stayed away from her for the most part—no one took the time to understand her. My father always said I reminded him of her, and I knew it wasn't a compliment—knew he thought there was something wrong with me, too. But that was later."

Mom rubs her hands, giving each of her palms a hard massage. Her hands are tired and cracked, her nails are still all jagged and bitten down. She stretches her fingers wide like they're thick bird wings and she is going to use them to fly away, but then she sighs and continues.

"The night Josephine was taking care of me, she set me on the floor and something bad was happening because she was screaming *No, No, Please no*. I couldn't see what was going on and couldn't move either. Her scared voice rang in my ears and the carpet smelled of metal and something left out to rot."

I can see Mom as a baby being held down by this fear, unable to say anything. It's the same feeling I've gotten when I read in the Guinness Book about people being buried alive, where no one can hear you, with nothing at all to do but lie there in the dark hoping for it to end. There was a community college student in Medford who was kidnapped and buried in a box underground for three whole days. It was on a TV special Mom let me watch when she was getting ready for a date with one of her boyfriends. I can't remember which one.

Sometimes in my closet now I have to leave the door open to make sure I'm not locked in and can get up and move around whenever I want. The knives in my stomach started to cut when Mom drove us downtown to where the bigger, nicer houses are, because one family had dug up their real grass and replaced it with plastic grass. All I could think of were the worms trapped underneath, not able to get back up to the air and sky and not understanding why. That's the worst part—no one even thinks to explain to the worms what is happening to their whole world.

Mom tells me she was born in the 1950s, and those weren't

the best years for being a kid—how the pediatrician told her parents not to hug her too much or at all, that too much affection was unhealthy for children.

"All the parents of that time had survived the Great Depression and World War II," she says, "They knew too much about scarcity and damage and wanted what they thought was a more practical approach."

There is Mom at three, with her arms extended upwards but no arms reaching back down.

"Things weren't explained to children back then," she continues. "When I had you, I wanted to make sure I explained things—explained things carefully and well. And I wanted you to have a lot of information so things weren't so scary, and to be able to feel a lot of feelings and for it to be okay. I wanted you to have that freedom. That's why I tell you so many things. I want you to know yourself and the world and to make your own decisions…" She drifts off. "But it's all been a lot harder than I thought."

The rain comes down now in heavy sheets and she gets up to see what's left for us to eat in the almost-empty fridge. I understand now that all the things she tells me are for a reason, that she is leading me somewhere on purpose.

"Gotta eat this before it goes to waste," she says, unwrapping cheese with green spots on it and carefully slicing off the moldy parts. Her hands catch my attention again, looking ancient to me, cracking in the webbed parts just like bird claws, like she is the only one getting older and I'm staying the same.

"What was it like when you had me?" I ask her, ignoring the food. She's gotten some bread and quince jam from the cupboard, too, and our unlit kitchen table sits before us—a haunted picnic.

"Well, before I had you, you kicked me in the stomach every morning at six a.m. You've always been a morning person,

Smokes." She gets up to put milk in a small pot, adds cinnamon, nutmeg, and honey, and turns it on low. She reaches up to the highest shelf to bring down a bag of cookies she's been hiding.

"The day of your actual birth was another rainy day, and I was alone. I was afraid I wouldn't be able to do it right and something would happen to you. The nurse was mean or maybe tired from her shift, and the lights were way too bright. I kept having the strange feeling that I wished I was outside in the dirt to give birth. I felt so awful that you were about to be forced to come out of all the warmth and darkness into that room's cold harshness. Luckily, the doctor was kinder and gentler than the nurse. He was older and told me you were going to be the one-thousandth baby he delivered. He said that was very lucky, an auspicious sign. But when he left me alone to go help his other patients the sheets smelled like loneliness. I was freezing in the thin robe and self-conscious about my genitals hanging out in the air. I was worried I was going to poop on the hospital table. It's a thing that can happen sometimes."

She smiles and wants me to smile, too, but this story is too sad and hard. Poor Mom doing this alone, and I wasn't born enough to help her yet.

"The mean nurse gave me a form where I had to fill out who the father was and *tsk-tsked* me when I put a line through the blank space. She thought I was a sinner or a future welfare mom or something. It didn't matter though, because there you were, coming out huge with your jet-black hair and thick rolls of fat—you even had rolls between your wrist and your elbow. I was glad you were so fat—made me believe you could make it through a natural disaster or something worse—that you could survive in this crazy world, easier than the less hefty babies."

I try to picture myself, thick with life. My arms now are two skinny sticks, not hefty but still strong enough.

"You asked me if you could have a brother, and you almost

did. He was one of the less hefty ones, and he decided not to stay. It's called a miscarriage. You were too young to remember, but Angela brought you to the hospital when I was there saying goodbye to him."

She has finished cutting the green spots off the cheese and puts a slice of what's left in her mouth. She starts to say something else but then keeps chewing.

"I wanted you, Smokey," she tells me after a pause, looking me straight in the eyes, making sure I'm listening. "Some people believe that before they're born, babies choose their parents—that they come back to Earth from the universe when they find the right human person to make them alive again. But for us, it was different. I chose you. I always had the unsettling sense that I made you come back here too early. And I'm sorry for that. I bet it was beautiful up there."

Outside someone's garbage can tumbles over in the wind and skids down the road.

"It's sometimes beautiful here, too—sometimes it's the best place to be," I tell her, and she looks down at her hands, then starts again.

"Others believe that humans come to Earth to suffer, to exist in bodies of bone and muscle and pain and desire, because up there it's all light and gorgeousness, and eventually that gets boring. We come here to experience all this weight, this gravity, this pain, this sharp ache. It kind of makes sense, doesn't it?"

Mom drifts off, in her own world now, but it does make sense to me, that we choose this. At this moment I know that she is the animal I choose, this is the small pack I was meant for—even with my loneliness, even with my stomach knives.

The lights flicker on and the fridge reluctantly starts humming again. The trees take a break from clawing at the roof. A crow lands on the outside windowsill and cocks its head at its own reflection. Mom lights her last Lucky Strike, and the gray air it makes moves up toward the ceiling as it always does. We watch the smoke rise and I imagine all the happy babies up there, so much farther up than our breath could ever travel, bathed in light and ease, eyeing all the future moms from a vast distance, far above the din.

Two-Rivers is a boy in my class who lives five blocks away from school. He says he has a pet squirrel and asks if I want to come over and meet it—that we could go that afternoon.

At Two-Rivers' house, there are lots of crooked steps to climb up to get to the front door. After we climb the steps, we are in a tree house that has thick, brown rental carpet like ours, and the heater cranked up. His mom pours us orange juice and says she doesn't know where the squirrel is right now, that it hasn't come out all afternoon.

Two-Rivers gets a can of nuts and shakes it, makes a *tchhh-tchhh* sound with his lips, and points to the top of the curtains, where on a wooden rod sits the squirrel, bushy tail twitching.

"See," he says, "Told ya.'"

"What's his name?" I ask, and Two-Rivers gives me a funny look.

"Just Squirrel," he says.

Squirrel jumps from one curtain rod to another one, hungry for the nuts. It jumps on to the back of the couch where Two-Rivers has made a trail of treats leading to him. It likes walnuts best. He puts a nut on his shoulder and the squirrel walks up his arm to get there, sniffs in his ear.

"You don't need to impress people with a pet squirrel to have friends," his mom says, standing in the doorway and watching him.

Two-Rivers pretends he doesn't hear her, and she sighs and goes back to the kitchen, rubbing her forehead like Mom does. When I say I have to go, he asks if he can come to my house the next day, that he can't bring Squirrel, but we could have fun anyways. And if not the next day maybe the day after that, or on the weekend, or anytime really. He has no way of knowing that I don't let anyone come to my house, don't want anyone to get that close, whether or not there is a boyfriend around, but especially not then. Even Toby has to wait for me outside, even when it's raining.

I climb back down his stairs without knowing how to explain this to Two-Rivers, this boy with so much hungry need on his face. At school, he starts looking sad around me, and then just stays away.

Mom slept somewhere else again last night, so I make my own cereal and cut in bananas, dump some brown sugar on top, and pour the milk carefully. I don't want any spills. She left a note saying she loves me and will be back in time to make us lunch. She drew two sandwiches in the corner: grilled cheese with tomato. Saturday cartoons are there behind the *On* button, but they will make everything worse—I'm too tired for their impossible reality—getting shot by Elmer Fudd and not feeling the blood leak out. Or running on air next to a steep cliff and still making it back to safety. I miss when cartoons used to be the most fun thing.

I haven't written in my journal yet. It's perfect as it is and my handwriting, my words, will come out and ruin everything. I flip through the pages and smell their clean softness. I find my special pen and the cap snaps off easily, like it's been ready and waiting for me this whole time. *Things you feel and notice and want*, Mom had told me, so I start there.

> *I feel the loneliness birds and the knives and the teeth and the wetness all around, under the floor and against the windowpane. I notice the old Polaroid of Mom before I was born and how small and happy she looks. I want to pack my school backpack full of hay and set Moon-shadow inside, want to walk out to the migrant camp and*

*say thanks for the music, thanks for everything, goodbye
everyone, then walk past the last road and into the dark
trees of the forest Mom says she will take me to someday.
I just can't wait for her. I want Deer to lead us there now,
want to follow in her hoof prints past everything I know
because she will understand exactly where to take me.*

I close the journal and give Moonshadow his pellets and a
carrot top. Out the window, there's frost on the ground and some
speckled gray birds at the suet feeder Mom put up a few weeks
ago.

"It's so they get strong and fat before winter," she told me,
and it sounded like she was a witch preparing to eat them herself. I pictured her plucking their downy feathers and smothering them in oil and garlic, setting them in the oven to broil on
high.

Past the feeder and across the street, Toby is out in his front
yard. If the temperature drops, Hanky-Panky makes him get
up and scrape the frost off the car windshield before he goes to
work. Toby told me that Hanky-Panky is even worse than his
dad, but didn't say how. He looked at the ground and rubbed his
face—he's been tired lately, coming to school with brown circles
under his eyes. Even the meaner kids are leaving him alone—
messing with someone so slow to react isn't as fun.

Toby's wearing red gloves and no shirt, revealing his white
chest, with blue pajama pants that are too small, so he looks like
a tall toddler. He turns my way and catches me watching him,
points his gloved hand to his head, and pretends that he is blowing his brains out. Hanky-Panky comes out and says something
to Toby, gets in his car and blasts heavy metal so loud as he peels
down the road that all the birds fly away. Toby shoots himself in
the head again, lets his tongue hang out of his mouth like a zom-
bie, and staggers up toward the door and inside.

After breakfast, I wander from room to room, pull out a box of Legos but don't want to make anything, don't want to build any square houses in square yards like you're supposed to. I turn on the heat and turn it off again. I pull out the painting Mom made. This other me looks calm and peaceful, hands folded and shoulders relaxed, but also more alone, with no Toby, no Moonshadow, no birds, and no Deer. And Mom is not there either, never was intended to be—she will always be out of the frame—the one creating all this from a distance.

I still don't have a head, doubt I ever will. All of Mom's paints and brushes are back in the basement. She has been more distracted again with not as much time to talk to me. She rushes around, leaves, returns, makes food, sleeps, needs her alone time. Even when she is right there doing dishes or writing the grocery list, she's also not there. She goes away more and more but I don't ask questions because I don't want to hear her answers.

I pull on my boots and a green jacket Mom got me at Goodwill—another thing off her list, she lets me know—since I outgrew my last warm coat. She says I'm growing up so fast and am going to be taller than her one day, but I can't imagine looking down at her, can't imagine being too grown to be carried around—her sack of apples, her scrappy creature.

I close the door behind me and head out the back, toward Old Oak. There's a well-worn path now, out past the laundry line and the fig trees, beyond the broken fence and into the meadow. It's not a straight line but a wandering, around tree stumps and blackberry vines, all naked and thorny with rotten berries turned darker than black, making patterns on the ground.

At the camp down the hill, light gray smoke rises from a fire but there's no music right now. Somebody clangs a pot that drowns out the sound of the low murmur of voices. I'm focused on the distance and don't hear the footsteps at first, so when I turn my head she's already so close. Deer is older now, not with her mother anymore. She chews the cold grass and eyes me, trying to remember. It feels like a long time since we ate blackberry leaves together, like a lot has happened.

The only other deer I've been this close to was a dead one. Mom pulled the car over to look at one that had been hit. She wanted to make sure it was all the way dead and not suffering.

"No one should suffer in pain for too long," she'd said, "death is better, more humane." But I don't know what she would do if it needed to be killed all the way, how she would do it.

The dead deer's eyes stared out into nothingness and its ribs did not move with breath. Its legs were broken, twisting back at sickening angles, but there was no blood anywhere. I started crying and Mom pulled me closer for a hug, but she didn't say anything to make it better. She didn't move us toward the car and away from there. We stood there together, and when I turned away from the deer, toward Mom, her eyes were closed and her lips were moving—she was saying a prayer, even though she doesn't know any.

Here in this clearing, my deer is alive and doing fine with her plump belly and clean coat. She is sure of herself, a little wary, but not afraid. I keep my body completely still, my breath coming out in quiet bursts of steam. She nibbles on a piece of green shooting up through the fallen leaves, and shivers—her body one delicate muscle, shimmering with dew.

I pick up a few leaves and draw my finger through the clay dirt in a line like it's cake frosting. In my mouth, it rests on my tongue until I have to swallow and then down it goes, filling me up in that same heavy, clean way, keeping my stomach teeth still. The weight of it makes me more a part of things—this is how I can stop floating up when I don't want to, this heft can help me stay here more easily, down on this earth, this dark soil.

—

Deer looks over my shoulder as a branch snaps, then bounds off, flying over downed logs and into the trees. In her place is Toby, come to find me.

"You're talking to deer now?" he asks from where he stands on his tippy-toes, kind of rocking himself. The brown hair sticking out from under his hat is greasy.

"Maybe," I say, and quickly wipe my mouth, hoping there's no mud there, no grit, worried he saw and knows of my secret feast, and something else unsettles me, too—this one thing is for me and no one else. This animal-becoming, this friendship with Deer is as private as taking a bath or the pulsing I sometimes get between my legs in my closet when everyone else is asleep. It is only for me.

He sits beside me, pulls a pocketknife out of his coat pocket, and picks up a stick to whittle.

"Hanky-Panky gave this to me," he says. "He wants to make me try to be more manly, like him."

I shrug—it's hard to tell what anyone really wants from anyone else.

"He should've thought twice before giving you a knife," I say, and he smiles, wipes the blade on his shirt sleeve, folds and unfolds it over and over, like he's making a new plan.

"I've also got these," he says, pulling out two plastic camo walkie-talkies.

They're made of flimsy plastic but have batteries already put in. When we turn them on the loud static makes us jump.

"Early Christmas present from my grandparents," he explains. "They're not coming to Christmas this year because they don't approve of Hanky, but they say maybe I can spend the summer with them. They say I need to get out of this place, that I could learn to ride horses if I want, could help out Grandpa and drive the tractors. The walkie-talkies are for us to use anytime, like if you have something important to say that can't wait. Or if there's ever an emergency..."

Imagining the things that could go wrong, about needing help, the walkie-talkies aren't quite as fun anymore, but maybe they could be useful. Toby gives me one and walks past the blackberry bushes and over a high mound of dirt.

"Over, over," he says.

"Over," I say and he tells me he's going a little farther away to find out how far apart we can be and still hear each other across the airwaves.

My green jacket keeps me warm while I'm waiting, even with cigarette burns on the sleeves, holes burned almost all the way through. Maybe the kid before me was a chain smoker like Mom, or maybe he was the ashtray.

I get up and walk out to the field toward the camp. There is no path, but the grasses aren't too high, and the rotting grains glisten with last night's rain. I want to get closer to the camp and find out if there are any kids our age. I've never seen any and that seems strange. I want to find out what it's like down there, up close.

"I can barely see you," Toby says. "Where are you going? That's too far."

Toby's voice sounds strange, kind of garbled, but not from static.

"Don't go so far," he says again, his voice rising. "Come back."

I look toward the camp again and there definitely aren't any kids. I'm disappointed and don't know why. Two men are jump-starting a truck and a woman is hanging clothing on a line.

I turn to head back up the hill toward Toby. The sun is casting its light directly above our heads—Mom might be back by now, making grilled cheeses, waiting and worried—or she could still be out wherever she goes, not thinking about me at all. I remember my future house full of animals in the wilderness, how Mom said she hoped I'd let her visit. I'm not sure anymore.

Toby stands in the distance behind some blackberry bushes with his pale face in his hands. His coat is buttoned up and his shoulders are shaking. His hat has fallen on the ground and his dark hair falls over his face, so he looks like a forest nymph trying to hide, but I'm the only one here.

"Are you okay?" I ask through the walkie-talkie.

It's the only thing I can think of to say.

There's only silence on the other end, then the kind of crying when someone is trying hard not to, but they can't stop the flood, and then a short blast of static before the line goes dead silent.

At the grocery outlet, Mom lets me push the cart, but the overhead lights sting my eyes. Mom gets tense at the store, trying to figure out how much of what we can afford, and keeps an extra bag of coins in her purse in case she comes up short with paper dollars. I park the cart in the vegetable area and go to get the eggs Mom wants. The breakfast cereal boxes flash their bright colors at me, but Mom gets us oatmeal to cook, says it is much more affordable, and besides, it makes no sense to give children sugar in the morning.

Around the corner from the eggs, I freeze. Mr. Kohl stands at the end of the aisle, a red, plastic basket hanging from his hand. He looks shorter here in the store, and his bald patch gleams shiny under the lights. He's talking to a woman and without thinking I look at his crotch, but everything is flat down there. I save this detail to tell Toby later.

I turn around to go down the next aisle to where the eggs live. Mr. Kohl is out of view but he's laughing at something the woman is saying. I open the carton of eggs and check to see if any are broken like Mom taught me. She wants me to leave the broken ones behind, but I leave them in the carton instead— otherwise, no one will want them—they'll sit here and rot, and the chickens will have done all that work for nothing. No broken ones this time, and I stop myself from opening up all the other cartons to make sure everyone is okay.

Back at the cart, Mom has loaded up on rice and frozen peas—says she has a new recipe to try—but I already know we will be using her bag of coins this time because these are the ingredients she buys when we are low on money.

In the produce aisle, Mom gets an apple, an orange, and a few lonely bananas, not the ones attached in a bunch like the others—maybe Mom does the same thing of making sure no one is left out. Another customer drops a kiwi on the floor and leaves it there, and as Mom pushes the cart toward check-out, I pick it up and put it back with the others. A few bins away, a red onion has ended up with the garlic, so I move that back to the others as well. My stomach knives start slicing because I might never be able to leave the produce section—there are too many beings separated from the rest, and they're lonely—and that's just not something I can walk away from. I put some grapes back in the bag with the others. Mr. Kohl is standing at the end of the row watching me with a strange look on his face.

"Hi, Smokey," he says. "Everything okay?"

I don't know what to say back and wonder how long he's been there, what exactly he's noticed.

The woman he's been talking to comes around the corner and puts a bottle of wine in his basket, and I know that either he already has or soon will put his penis inside her. I don't understand why anyone would let Mr. Kohl do that, why people do that ever or at all.

Once I heard Mom tell Angela—as they sat at the kitchen table, Angela's permed and gelled auburn hair looking plastic under the overhead light—that she liked to sleep with men with big, hairy bellies so she could have something to rub up against. That was the day I stopped eavesdropping on Mom and Angela.

"My mom is waiting for me," I say, and when I am a few feet past them, I apologize silently to all the fruits and vegetables I didn't have a chance to help, and promise them I'll do better next time. I hope my lips aren't still moving the way they do some-times when I think they're not.

I hear the woman say to Mr. Kohl in a loud whisper, "What a strange little kid," as Mom waves me over and asks where I've been. She pulls out her bag of coins and we wait and wait for the cashier to count out all those dull nickels and pennies.

Outside, three crows sit on the handle of a grocery cart and watch us as we load the bags into the trunk.

"I have an idea," Mom says, with the shopping over and her tenseness gone.

We drive past a liquor store, a bar, and a military supply shop, turn onto State Street and drive west, past houses that sit back on their haunches, mangy and wet. We drive past the drive-thru with the yellow duck on the sign, over the Mill Creek bridge, to downtown. The stores here are warm red brick and sturdy, with nice things to look at—soap and fresh bread for sale, bouquets of flowers, toys, books, hot coffee, bicycles—all lined up in the store windows. Mom isn't talking and I'm not either. The radio is off and it's just us and our thoughts—the sound of our own breathing. I roll down my window and the cool air fills my nose and chest.

Mom turns south now, along railroad tracks and a black body of water, fringed by stalks of reeds. She keeps going over some speed bumps, past a fishing shack, and finally, parks under the biggest oak tree I've ever seen.

"I can't believe I haven't brought you here before now," she says, and I can't believe it either.

We get out and shut the car doors behind us. The sound of the metal echoes like a gunshot in this forest of oaks, but the calls of birds quickly take over—crows and red-winged black-birds and a low prehistoric squawk that Mom says is a Great Blue Heron. We walk along a trail by a creek, past the towering trees to an open meadow, sit on the damp ground, and say nothing.

We don't need to—before us is a stage and we are the watchers. Mom points to a fallen tree in the distance and keeps pointing until I look closely enough to see what she sees: it's where the Great Blue Heron decided to land. He is huge and beautiful with his back of silver-blue feathers and a black swoop above his eye.

"Maybe we will get to watch him catch a fish," she whispers.

Smaller birds flit from tree to tree, their brown backs soft and delicate. They fly over to land on reeds that sway in the wind and talk to each other across the meadow. The sun is starting to set, and the dimming lights make a show for us, blues and purples and reds all fading to a pink that settles over everything.

I expect Mom to say something about getting the groceries home, that we should head back so she can make dinner, or that she has plans later and I'll need to put myself to bed. Instead, she just sits quietly with her eyes closed, and the darkening colors make shadows across her pinkened skin as the last of the birds quiet down for the night. Even the heron has blended into all that surrounds him.

*"Tomorrow I turn twenty-nine," Mom says, but the dark cir-*cles under her eyes make her seem like a tired child, like how Toby comes to school sometimes. He says ghosts come in the night when he can't sleep and try to push his eyes closed so hard, they sometimes leave bruises. When I asked him how come he doesn't just shut his eyes himself, he says he can't—it's his job to stay awake in case something bad happens—he has to be ready. I understand what he means.

Mom says, "The number twenty-nine is all about change and progress and taking action." She rubs her forehead and smiles weakly at me, "Maybe this will be my year."

When she grabs her purse and says she is going to get a cup of coffee with Angela real quick, I use a stool to get paper and pens from the cupboard. I grab a ruler, too—I want these birthday gifts to be perfect. The first coupon is for a shoulder rub. The second one is for making her pancakes since I know how to do that now. The third one is the one I think she will like the most— she can just hand it to me without talking and when she does I will know to go away to leave her alone for a whole hour. She won't even have to ask—she won't need to waste her breath at all.

The phone doesn't ring very often at our house, and when it does, one or both of us jumps, startled by its unexpected shrillness. Mom raises her eyebrows in a question and goes to find out who it is. I can't make out the caller's voice on the other end, just that it's a man. Mom's forehead is creased and she nods and says *Mmm-hmmm* and keeps looking at me across the room. "Hmmm," she says, "I'll keep an eye out," and then, "Things are fine here at home, yes."

When she sets the phone back in the cradle and the click of it echoes in the kitchen, Mom says it was Mr. Kohl calling, that he wanted to check in, make sure everything was okay here.

I am sure now he saw me talking to the fruits and vegetables at the store, and wonder what else he's noticed. Maybe he saw me looking at his crotch like Toby. Maybe he saw Mom at the store and wants to date her like all the other men do, and his call wasn't about me at all. Men will do a lot of things to try to get to Mom.

"Everything's fine," I say, and she tells me to make sure I tell her if there's ever anything going on. I think of White Richard and Jerome and Claudio, of the crying and the thuds and the knives, but I doubt Mr. Kohl would want to know about any of that.

"Did he ask you out?" I ask, and she turns around with her brow creased but also a small smile pulling at her lips.

"Of course not," she says, "What a strange question."

She goes back to what she was doing as the rain keeps coming down. Our basement has a creek running through it now, smelling like tarnished silver, like silt. Drowned mice are belly-up on the stairs, and outside their gray bodies are soaked through, pushed up and out of their hiding places with the rising waters. Along the driveway and in the grass of the front yard they are laid out like we are having a funeral, their pink feet curled into themselves. I put on my boots and grab our shovel to bury each one, but I'm running out of places to dig. Mom helped out at first, but now is tired of it—she is tired of everything. The new boyfriend she told me about has vanished, my wishes granted, but a wide, blue sadness covers everything anyway. From a distance, the dead mice on the bright green grass look like strange Easter eggs, abandoned and rotting in their too-easy hiding places.

"Their bodies need to go back into the earth. We have to keep going," I say, but Mom just shakes her head and closes her eyes.

She doesn't move or say anything as I go back out alone to bury all the ones I can find. She watches me from the window as I dig the holes. I scoop out dirt with the shovel and apologize to each one as the mud covers it.

I'm sorry, I'm sorry, I'm sorry.

One of them is still alive, but barely. His small mouth is open and he gasps for air, his body moving with slow shudders until he takes one last breath and goes still. I smooth down his gray fur with my finger, and apologize to him, too.

"I'll put you by the fig tree," I tell him, and scoop him up gently in case he can still feel the earthly feelings.

After he and the others are buried, I head back inside and take off my boots. Mom says to make sure I wash my hands with extra soap and I shake the rain out of my hair like a dog.

"You need a haircut," she says from the kitchen table where

she's drawn a picture of a mouse on the back of a coaster she brought home from some bar.

She motions me over and moves her warm fingers through my wet hair—her gentle hands are strong and sure, even as her eyes are sad enough that she might start crying any minute.

In the bathroom mirror, I pull all my hair back so my forehead goes tight, and imagine it all gone. What I most want is for her to shave it all off, to watch each dark curl fall to the cold floor like sad confetti, leaving me clean and new, a more streamlined creature left with only bone and muscle and nothing else to slow me down.

"Have you ever shaved your head?" I ask her, back in the kitchen, trying to picture her as a shorn sheep.

"God, no," she says laughing. "Remember Mrs. Boogey?"

She should know I will never forget Mrs. Boogey. She sleeps under the Marion Street Bridge. Mom says she was probably released from the mental hospital and didn't have anywhere else to go. When I was five, I started picking my nose and couldn't stop, even though I knew it was gross—an embarrassment to Mom and to myself. She told me hundreds of times to knock it off and threatened various punishments—no cartoons, no dessert, no nothing—but I couldn't stop myself.

She put me in the car one morning when I was still in pajamas and drove down to the bridge. We parked and waited, and Mom wasn't talking, wouldn't say anything, just had a grim look, like she had to do this thing and nothing was going to stop her. It wasn't too long before Mrs. Boogey appeared. Her hair was pulled out in clumps, her bald scalp scabbed over on one side, reflecting back the gray light coming through the clouds. The orange coat she wore hung off her skeleton body. On her left foot, she wore a big, black combat boot, on her right a blue sneaker with no laces. Her pants were the worst—stained a deep, dark brown at the crotch, ripped open at the knee.

Her hands moved mechanically, right on cue. I looked at Mom and knew why she'd brought me there. With one hand and then the other, her fingers jabbed and scraped deep into her nostrils, followed by a frenetic licking of what came out, over and over like she'd never be able to stop.

I pictured her as a kid my age, named Stephanie or Megan, with parents and a house, going to school and getting A's— but none of it mattered now. Here she was alone, in wet, dirty clothes, under this cement bridge, with no one around to help her, and just her own snot to eat for dinner. Mom wanted to show me how I could end up if I didn't get my own problem under control.

I haven't picked my nose once since then, but a couple times Mom must have thought I was going to, because from where she sat in the living room or on the front steps all she had to say was *Mrs. Boogey* and I stopped what I was doing, transported straight back to her, all wet and cold out there, alone in her picked-apart body, with her dirty fingers and scabby scalp.

"You wouldn't look like Mrs. Boogey with a shaved head," I say.

"You wouldn't either. And you're going to have a beautiful life, baby," she tells me. "Don't think about Mrs. Boogey too much. Taking you to see her was just another of my very bad parenting decisions."

I choose an old, stained towel from the drawer, wrap it around my shoulders and sit on the kitchen stool. Mom has her sharpest scissors out and puts on her Joni Mitchell record. It's the one where Joni is on the front smoking a cigarette and wearing a black beret. Mom has the same beret but doesn't wear it very often. The rain outside makes a chorus that goes along with each of the songs.

Every scissor snip is a lightening-up, a freeing. Each curl tumbles toward the blue and white linoleum while her hands work above each ear, at the front and at the nape, the metal sure against my skin, and it feels like a kind of medicine. Joni's voice sends high notes down my spine and the patter of the rain outside is the sound of home.

When Mom rubs my head and takes the towel off, my job is to sweep up all the hairs, take them outside, and set each wisp in a tree branch for the birds to make their nests. It was something her grandmother taught her once, something she did back in Texas. She told me that by the time her grandmother died at ninety-nine, all the birds' nests in the neighborhood and even beyond were soft and white, that they glowed silver in the moonlight. Outside, I place my hair in different tree branches, and tell the blue jays and robins and house sparrows that it's all for them.

Back inside Mom laughs because I haven't even looked in the mirror yet. I go to the bathroom and can't believe she's done this thing. I run my hands over my cropped head, holding my breath. I am a sleek seal, an ocean swimmer, a shorn lamb. I am a real boy now, sturdy and tough. I feel the most right I've felt in a long time, and Mom is smiling behind me and giving me a hug, and my stomach knives are completely still, like they've been washed and dried and put away in a drawer closed so tight they are going to lose all their sheen.

"Let's try to finish the painting before it grows out," she says. She hasn't abandoned the portrait after all. "Maybe when the rain lets up."

I nod and run my hands over my head again. Mom says she's running me a bath so I can get all the tiny hairs off. She puts in bubbles.

I climb into the tub, and she gets a washcloth to clean my neck, shoulders and back, and rinses off my collarbone. Her touch is gentle, but something has shifted; a growing tension making all the bubbles pop.

"Remember how I told you about Gary?" she asks, and my

stomach sinks, my gnashing teeth always ready to wake up when the time is right.

"I thought you got rid of him," I say, and she looks confused, then frowns. "I thought he wasn't going to come around after all."

"He can't quite yet but will very soon," she says, "but you'll meet him on Saturday. We're going to go visit him."

I ask if we are going to his house and she says, "Not exactly." Mom doesn't want to talk anymore. She rubs shampoo into my scalp and tells me to close my eyes as she uses the bucket to rinse me clean.

"Have you been writing in your journal? It's okay if you haven't." Before I can answer she says, "Making art is the only thing I respect about myself."

I want to be one of her art projects, one of the things she feels good about making. She lifts the bucket to give me one more rinse.

Mom leaves me to go turn on the heater that snaps and crackles to life. If you look down into it there is a tangle of wires, glowing orange. I wrap the towel around my body and head to my closet, put on pajamas. I pull out the journal and pen again. I count the number of pages, the number of words I've written so far, the number of freckles on my right arm, then my left arm. Tomorrow I'll meet Gary. Maybe he will like me, teach me things—boy things that Mom doesn't know about or have time for. I count how many boyfriends I can remember. I count how many days in a row it has been raining. I count how many black and white penguins are on my pillowcase. I count how many toes I have even though I already know. Feel, notice, and want.

I feel the sleep coming, and notice that the spider who lives in my closet has dropped down lower than usual. He wants to know how he can help. He hangs by an invisi-

ble string, floating back and forth as my breath pushes him. He knows he can trust me, understands I won't hurt him. Talking to him with my voice would be too loud for his small ears so I talk to him with my mind. You're okay here. You belong here, too. No one will hurt you. Satisfied, he nods and crawls back up his string to the uppermost corner, maybe for a late-night snack. He calls me by my real name, says he's going to watch out for me tonight and for all the nights he can. I want to make my own invisible string, a silver rope, that I can climb up into some hidden place. I will try to start learning how in the morning.

I write Gary's name nine times at the bottom and close the journal. Mom said nine is the number that means both magic and the end of something. She told me about nines because that's how old I'll be soon, but all I want is for nines to mean the end of Gary. I set my journal out into the hallway so maybe Mom will find it. I hope she will be curious and read what I've written so far and understand she has to change her mind.

Rain hits the roof harder and the creek water in the basement below us picks up more speed, drowning more mice but also the laundry hamper and my bicycle, too, a rising tide that we can't do anything about, except move what we can lift to higher ground, and wait.

Those mouse bodies out there in their shallow graves might all be on the grass again in the morning, belly-up once more, their tiny pink feet a cold gray—curled and clenched. From now on, for the rest of my life, I'll spend every morning burying them and every night preparing for their return, until I'm as old and alone and sad as Mom is—until all that's left of any of us are the tiniest of bones that the crows will find and take away like jewels.

It's the worst when Mom tries to hide her crying, when she places the palm of her hand on the top of my head for a moment and keeps walking, past where I sit on the couch, to her room. She closes the door behind her, and I can hear the sigh of her bed on the floor as she lies down. I picture her curled into a ball—like a potato bug, like a knot—when the tears come, her hands clenched into fists or maybe rubbing at her eyes—her head on the pillow where all her tears will be soaked up and saved for later. She is sad and there is nothing I can do about it. The men bring the tears, and they take them away. I turn on the TV to the sound of fake laughter and wait.

On Saturday, Mom says there's no time for cartoons and burns the scrambled eggs she's made for us. I push them around my plate without trying to hide it, wanting her to know how unhappy I am. Mom's too nervous to notice or eat—she keeps checking herself in the mirror and even puts on lipstick. She almost looks like a little, brown-haired Ronald McDonald but she's not smiling big enough.

She packs a lunch, and we get in the car and drive through a neighborhood I've never seen before.

"It's called Felony Flats," Mom says as we pass crooked porches and junked cars with their hoods propped open, a toddler in diapers playing with a tire pump in the yard. "When I was in high school a friend of mine lived right there," she tells me, pointing to a sad, brown house with moss and prehistoric-looking green ferns taking over the roof. "I wonder what happened to her."

Beyond the houses is a wide asphalt area with no trees at all. The sky's thick, gray clouds hover over the parking lot next to the tall cement blocks of what Mom calls the *minimum-security facility*, a place for locking people up who have done bad things but not the worst things. The barbed wire leading to the jail yard looks loosely done, as if someone hasn't bothered to make the tension hold and the wire is just for show—no one is going to try too hard to get in or out.

"You're sure Gary wants to meet me?" I ask Mom again.

I asked her this last night, too. She nods now but hasn't really heard me, and turns the radio on and off as we sit in the parking lot. I tell her I hope he is different from the others, and she says she hopes so, too. I think of Kaleb and all the air goes out of my chest. I still miss him, even though he's never coming back—I know it for sure now. She squeezes my shoulder and tells me to grab the lunch from the backseat. I want to ask her where she's been going at night if he's in here. I want to ask why she always leaves. I want to ask how she met Gary, ask how long he's been locked up, and if maybe he'll stay in there until I'm a grown-up. By then I'll have moved away to my wilderness home and Mom can be with gray Gary, his face and arms probably the same color as all these cement blocks surrounding us.

Mom told me that Gary is in for robbery. He took things from old people when they were sleeping to get money to buy narcotics. Mom says he never hurt the old people so I don't need to be concerned and explains that narcotics are drugs that make your mind and body numb so you can't feel anything for a while. She says it's not Gary's fault he got addicted.

"Sometimes the pain of being alive is too much," she says.

Maybe the narcotics could make my stomach teeth and all my feelings numb, too—make the tiny knives stop their cuts. I will ask Toby if he knows anything about them.

In the visiting room, the guards near the doors wear tight, tan pants and their penis lumps are clear outlines of zucchinis, cucumbers, and bananas. They have button-down shirts tucked into black leather belts and sturdy work boots they keep polished and shiny. Their muscular, hairy arms are too large for their shirt sleeves, and I keep waiting to hear the rip of torn fabric when they reach for their clipboards and pens. There is a vending machine with a cracked front that for a dime will shoot out a paper cup with spades, diamonds, hearts, and clubs printed on the sides.

The last card needed for a set or a run is underneath, but Mom only gave me one dime so I haven't had a chance to win yet.

The visiting room has the look and feel of the YMCA, with paint peeling off the walls and no money for heating. In the center of the room sits a heavy pool table with worn-down green felt that can withstand the weighted leans of large, tattooed men.

When Gary comes in through a thick door, he does not want to meet me. He doesn't even look in my direction. He only has eyes for Mom—hard eyes like he is a hungry wolf who understands he won't be eating for a while. Mom tells me they need their alone time but that she put a deck of cards in my lunch box: Solitaire again.

She says I can eat the sandwich she packed whenever I get hungry. I look in the bag and find that Mom got me a treat—not the usual whole wheat—instead, the starched white Wonder Bread that I've only had once, when Toby shared part of his sandwich with me. He said it's what the astronauts eat when they go on their space missions, and it made sense. Sitting on the bench near the barred windows, the bologna and lettuce stick to the roof of my mouth, and I keep my eyes on Mom and Gary. I'm on an alien planet in my space suit—a speck of light far off in the distance.

A man in one of the orange jumpsuits comes over and leans down to my level, eye to eye, and introduces himself as Amos. He is lean, with tattoos of ships and anchors on his skinny arms, all the blue ink fading back into his dry, cracked skin. He follows my eyes to where Mom and Gary sit, holding hands and either laughing or crying, I'm not sure which.

"Lovebirds are the worst," he says, rolling his brown eyes with a smile like he understands my situation exactly.

Amos is in here, but he is more of a songbird than a regular man, light on his feet and bright like the house sparrows that come to our yard. I can't imagine him having done anything terrible enough to get locked up, can't imagine him stealing from sleeping old people.

"I grew some plants I wasn't supposed to," he says, reading my mind. "I wasn't hurting anyone—it was for medicine. I miss those plants, but most of all I miss my dog. I hope he's okay. My cousin is supposed to be looking out for him while I'm in here."

I know he is talking more to himself than to me when he says that, but when I blink, there is Bingo—tied up alone outside, even when the ground is frozen—his sad eyes following me when I pass. I try to concentrate and tell him with my mind that someone will rescue him, and that I hope that someone will be me—that I will try to find a way.

I understand what Amos means about missing his plants, too. I want to be beneath Old Oak's branches right now, taking deep gulps of fresh air.

"Want to learn how to shoot pool until your Mom's done?" he asks me.

He waves at her across the room to check if it is okay, but she doesn't look away from Gary.

I tell Amos it's fine, and at the pool table, he shows me how to check if the cue is straight enough by rolling it across the felt, explains angles and momentum. The other men in the room are friendly, too, and when they learn my name is Smokey they all say what a smooth name that is. They smile down at me but there's something sad behind their grins—maybe they're missing their own kids, their old lives. I don't understand why Mom chose Gary when there are other men here who could be so much better for us—I know they're good, because my stomach knives aren't sending up any red alerts. Any one of these other ones would do. Why doesn't she understand that?

"Hey, Smokey," Amos says during a break in the game when most of the guys go off to smoke cigarettes or talk to the guards. "Can I tell you a secret?"

One of the knives in my stomach moves up and down then, a sharp jab. Mom has told me many times that secrets are something to watch out for, especially when they come from an adult. I don't say anything at first. Amos's angular shoulders stick out from his shirt, and he runs his hands through his feathered hair while he waits for my answer.

I look over at Mom, holding Gary's hands in hers and smiling at him wider than she's smiled in weeks, looking more like Ronald McDonald by the second. But then I see what's underneath her smile and fight the urge to run over and hug her. She is desperate to keep the loneliness birds away. She believes Gary can help. From across the room, I see she has smeared her lipstick.

I look away from her and up at Amos and nod *Yes* that he can tell me. He says he's been sneaking Wonder Bread from the cafeteria back to his cell; he's discovered that if he molds it carefully, it will hold its shape, eventually hardening into something cement-like.

"I'm almost finished with a complete chess set but I need a few more pawns," he explains, smiling his gentle sparrow smile.

Mom stands up then and waves me to her, because Gary's visiting time is over. Her eyes are red and puffy, but she smiles at Amos, tells him thank you, and asks me to go get my stuff. I leave the rest of my sandwich out on the bench, and nod to Amos so he understands it's for him. The guards are playing checkers and drinking coffee, but one of them gets up to let us out. He's got jet-black hair and a curved banana right at eye level. He winks at me as we open the door and step out.

When Toby asks what I did over the weekend, I tell him I spent part of it in prison and he is impressed. We never talked about what happened in the field with the walkie-talkies, how when I went over to him in the blackberry bushes to check if he was okay, he told me to leave him the hell alone. When I left him there to go home, Mom had made us grilled cheese sandwiches as promised, but wouldn't talk about where she'd been the night before, and said it didn't matter because she came back and everything is fine.

In the kitchen, I take out a couple of pieces of the rest of the Wonder Bread to save for Amos when we go to visiting hours next Saturday, but Gary gets released on Tuesday while I'm at school. I come home to find him at our kitchen table. He's a freed wolf now, eating a big plate of chicken enchiladas Mom has made for him. I watch him and understand I won't get to say goodbye to Amos, won't get to deliver more bread to him. I don't want to eat it now either—my astronaut mission is over early. I decide to let it sit there, wasted and hardened for no purpose at all, until Mom gets around to throwing it out.

Moonshadow chewed the edges of my journal. Now it looks like something from a treasure chest, ancient and important. *Feel and notice and want.*

I'm afraid of a lot of things—these minefields, these aches. The grown-ups aren't having any fun, and the kids aren't either. I don't know what the animals are feeling, but they are doing something that makes more sense than all this. The ants and the spiders, the raccoons, Moonshadow and the deer: they understand the thing that I want to understand. I want to spend more time low to the ground. I think that's part of it. I want to scratch at the dirt and smell everything, cover up my scent, and hide my tracks. I want to drink from the rivers where they're still clean— not like Moss River with its dirty water, with its mills and factories. I want my animal body. I want to get it back.

I keep having dreams about someone I think is Great-Aunt
Josephine. In my dreams she sits at a round table and tells people their fortunes. Her hands are slender with long, white fingers and dirt under her nails. She's got her Ouija board and she's calling the spirits. Right before I wake up, I realize I'm a spirit, and she's trying to tell me a secret that might make me feel better.

Mom is sometimes willing to talk about her and sometimes she isn't.

"She was very beautiful, but in an unusual way," Mom tells me this morning—a dry morning with a bright blue sky. "She was the tallest woman in our family and very slender. I could wrap my hand around her whole wrist easily, even when I was little. She didn't talk much. Kind of like you."

"But did she see the spirits in the Ouija? Were people afraid of her?"

"My dad was afraid of her, said she'd been strange her whole life, even when they were little kids. Your Grandpa Jack was very straight-laced and had a mean streak, so I don't think they ever got along. He did feel remorseful later when she disappeared."

"What do you mean?" I asked, though this made sense in a way. This is why I'd never met Great-Aunt Josephine. Where had she been all this time?

"When she was around twenty, she told the family she was going to study on the east coast, in upstate New York, with one of the spiritualist churches there. She wanted to devote her life to talking to the dead. Of course, nobody here understood. But she had saved money and no one could stop her—maybe were even relieved she was leaving. It's just that we never got word—after one postcard she sent from a train station in Pennsylvania, that was it. No one heard if she ever even made it upstate."

"Maybe she's still there. Maybe she's happy now," I say, imagining her escape from these people who didn't understand or like her much.

"It's possible," Mom said. "It's what I would like to believe. She's the one who taught me about the numbers, too, about how they mean things. She taught me that everything you can notice means something. Even the leaves in your tea. You would have really liked her. She was special."

I imagine her visiting Moss River and taking me away with her when she returned east—maybe she would see I understand things, too. She would use her magic to fit me into her suitcase, and we would fly across the country together on the back of a raven. She would explain everything about the numbers and the other signs, tell me the secret of what happened that day when Mom was a baby and something scared them both—maybe that's the key to everything bad that has happened since—it is a riddle, and solving it will break this dark spell of us.

I don't tell Mom that Great-Aunt Josephine has been coming to me at night, that I've watched her long, white fingers move through space and rest on my shoulder, felt her realness beside me like help from afar.

Narcotics Anonymous meetings with Mom and Gary are held in a rundown, dark-green duplex off Milltown Road, where a living room full of kids eat stale cookies and watch Michael Jackson's "Thriller" video over and over. Mom says coming here is a condition of Gary's parole and she wants us to be supportive, but all I want is for him to get away from us—back to jail or anywhere else.

In the corner of the room, at a wobbly table, an older boy waves me over. He says his name is Houdini and tells me to split the deck of cards he holds in half. One of his teeth in the front has a dark gray sheen, and his skinny body is all elbows and knees. Houdini doesn't talk much but shuffles the tattered deck and asks me to point to a card. He shows me its face and puts it back in the deck. I want to watch the trick but have to keep an eye out in this room—something has gone wrong here—disappointment is soaked into the couch cushions like so much spilled Dr. Pepper, and no adults are in sight if something goes wrong. There's a little girl on a beanbag chair holding her crotch like she has to pee but there's no one to take her, and a boy using the tip of a ballpoint pen to carve his initials into the wall by the door. It's too dark in this room, everything a shadow.

"Is this your card?" Houdini asks me.

I say it is so he can be proud of his trick, but I can't be sure. I have started floating up and can't remember if I picked an eight of clubs or an eight of spades.

"Thriller" starts again at the beginning on the old brown TV. I don't want to admit to this Houdini boy, or anyone else, that Michael Jackson's quick hip thrusts, his girlfriend's fearful face, and the stilted zombies send rivers of dread through me, because when I look around, I'm not the youngest one in the room. Besides the crotch-holding girl, there are other kids younger than me sitting on flattened, musty beanbags chairs and staring at the screen with their eyes wide open, unbothered.

When the adults come out from behind the closed door where sometimes there is crying and sometimes yelling and sometimes no sounds at all, they throw back the last of their black coffee. They are shipwreck survivors with salty, bloodshot eyes. We kids are young sailors on unsteady sea legs, desperate for land, scrambling to get our things and be the first to get out of there. Only Houdini doesn't move. He continues shuffling his cards as if being here is better than what comes next—I think he might already know something that I am just starting to learn. Gary, Mom, and I walk out to the car, and in our silence I can still hear Michael Jackson through the screen door, can picture his red pants thrusting and thrusting as he sings and dances with the zombies, over and over, on repeat forever.

It's not too long before Gary stops being willing to go to the NA meetings, even though he promised. When Gary punches the refrigerator door, slamming his fist into it over and over, Mom explains to me how difficult it is for addicts to stay clean. Now Mom has to find a way to replace the refrigerator, but we are extra broke because Gary can't get a job, and he eats more than Mom and I put together, filling the sink with dirty dishes and leaving spots of meat grease on the countertop and in tracks across the floor. Mom talks to me about the refrigerator and explains how credit cards work but doesn't talk about the split in her lip, the yellowing bruises on her back I saw when she stepped into the shower with the door open, or her new jumpiness, startling in her chair with any sound—even the accidental drop of a spoon.

When he gets me alone, Gary says I look like a *lesbo-faggot* with my short haircut and overalls, and he uses his open hand to hit me on the back of my head when I don't say anything back. Gary wants a fight. He hits me hard enough that a dull ache blooms there as my neck gives out and my head snaps forward. He says he knows I'm going to grow up to be a *sick-in-the-head-queer* and says he has seen me looking at his dick through his jeans. Sometimes when Mom is in the other room, he catches my eye and points to his crotch, smiling a mean smile.

I can't eat anything now. I'm an expert at pushing food from one side of my plate to the other and leaving the table early because my stomach knives are sharper than ever. Lately, I bleed when I go to the toilet. It's getting worse but I still don't want to tell Mom—she needs to go to the hospital more than I do, every day a new injury. If both of us go to the clinic now, everyone will know we have failed, and they'll get out their clipboards and write things down—about us and what to do about us—and it won't be good. Now that Gary has moved in, I stand or sit with my back to the wall so I can always keep an eye on things. I'm not sure what he hits Mom with, but from the other side of the wall it sounds less like my thuds and more like something sharper—almost metallic—and I can taste the blood.

Tonight, Gary has been drinking clear liquid from a large bottle that makes the whites of his eyes pool with red. He stumbles in the doorway and finds the unfinished painting Mom started of me. He brings it to where Mom and I sit together, her arm wrapped around me as we read *The Animal Family* because Mom is trying to make things normal. I look at my headless body.

"What the fuck is this?" he says, holding it up and laughing like it's the stupidest thing he's ever seen. I look at the greens and browns surrounding my shoulders and remember how it felt that day, to be seen and appreciated.

My whole body goes taut and I want to kill him, gouge his eyes out, slice him open with a kitchen knife or Toby's screwdriver, want to protect Mom and her painting, protect Moonshadow, protect everyone from Gary and men like Gary. Mom wants someone to love her, but she can't catch a break. He is about to smash the framed canvas over his knee or throw it against the wall but changes his mind—watches us watching him and sets it down, already forgotten, and throws the now-empty bottle at the wall behind us instead. It shatters and sprays glass onto the couch. Moonshadow pokes his head out from where he's hiding behind a potted plant and Gary stomps the floor in his direction, mutters something about how he'd taste *fucking delicious with a side of potatoes* before stomping back to the bedroom where he slams the door and waits.

From Mom's room he yells *Shit! Shit! Fuck this shit!* over and over, and Mom is crying hard. I'm crying too because I know there's no way out of this. She is going to go back there to calm him down, and I can't do anything about it—can't even speak—because I've floated up to the ceiling where I watch her pull her arm out from around me and set the book down. She wipes the tears from her eyes and promises me it will all be okay.

She says to go into the bathroom and lock the door, run a bath so the sound of the water covers up the other sounds. I lure Moonshadow out from his hiding place with a piece of celery and take him with me, undress in the cold and turn the water on high, let it wash over my shaking hands while I get the temperature right. I submerge my body down into the tub as the steam rises like clean smoke. I tilt my head back so my nose and mouth are out of the water but my ears are under. All the sounds are jumbled like listening to a movie from somewhere far away.

I touch my bird skeleton—bony collarbone, bony hips, and bony feet—remembering that I have skin and hair and eyes, that I'm an animal who belongs to an animal family and who needs to try to stay here on Earth. I press my hands against my skull, remember that I do have a head, that it's attached right here above my neck. The realization is a reminder—I'm not the flat person in Mom's painting, I am just unfinished. I submerge my whole body under, holding my breath, keeping track of how high I can count, imagine opening my mouth and nose to suck in water in a whoosh and, if I did, how it could all be over like it was for little Noah, no one to hear and no one to come pull me out. The only one left would be beautiful Moonshadow stretched out on the bathmat. I pull myself up from below the surface, chest heaving. Moonshadow scratches behind his ear and licks his black paw, tells me to just keep breathing, and shows me how.

When the tub is close to overflowing and the tap is off, sounds from Mom's room creep through the walls and there's crying now, but no hits and no shoves. Crying is what comes at the beginning and at the end. There's a slow and steady storm building in my stomach, knives and teeth, and black tar solid-ifying in a dark, wet place. I get out of the bathtub and barely make it to the toilet in time, everything coming out the texture of ground coffee with red flecks, heaving and heaving beyond when there's nothing left, then a forced trickle of the dirty water coming up out of my throat and the smell of something burnt. I flush away this heavy, now-familiar secret and lay down on the cold bathroom floor next to Moonshadow, wipe the sick from my mouth, and close my eyes.

"Smokey, open the door," Mom whispers later, the sky dark through the window, with no stars out and no sounds. "It's me, it's okay."

When I open the door, I might be sick again. Her face is more busted up than it's ever been, but she tells me not to be afraid. She glances at the toilet and I'm glad I flushed everything down so she doesn't have to worry more—she doesn't need this extra problem.

"Your face," I say, and she shushes me, turns off the bath-room light, and sits down so we are on the floor together in the dark. She rubs my back and presses a damp washcloth against her torn-up cheekbones.

Moonshadow brushes past to go back to the closet and Mom covers me with a towel and holds my hand, walking with me in her bare feet even though the heater broke and it's so cold our breath is all ghosty.

"I'm going to sleep in here with you tonight," she says. "We haven't done that in a while."

—

We climb onto my narrow mattress under the blankets, and Mom hums a song she used to sing when I was a baby. *There's a wee little moon lying on his back with his little tiny toes in the air. And he's all by himself in the great, big sky but the funny little moon doesn't care.*

She falls asleep before I do. I can hear her breath fall into its rhythm as her muscles loosen into rest.

I wish she understood that she should have brought Amos home to live with us instead, imagine Amos as my new father— making his pawns and rooks, teaching me about the eight ball and other lessons he learned—how to trust someone with a secret, what it means to be kind, and other gifts he gathered up in his sculptor's hands.

He's so far away now behind that loose barbed wire. He's out there under a canopy of overwintered sycamores, roots rotting in the rain and looking so dead that they won't ever sprout green again.

This afternoon Gary rolls up on a black motorcycle, the silver parts rusty and the whole thing rattling the windows and our teeth. He says his friend loaned it to him and we are all going on a joy ride. Mom asks about helmets and Gary says we're just going down the road and back, for us both to get on and that it will be fun. Mom climbs on behind him and I climb on behind her, my whole body tightened into a knot—I don't want to keep getting left behind, but I don't want to go either. I want there to be a third choice that no one has thought of yet.

Mom tells him to go slow, but he revs the motor three times and takes off, Mom holding on to him while my own arms reach around Mom's skinny waist, frantic to find something steady to hold on to, but I don't find much. I close my eyes as the motor growls below me, Gary lets out a whoop, and we race over potholes and past the trailer park to a gravel turn-around where he skids us to a stop.

He looks behind him to see my scared face and says *I'm a fucking baby who is never any fun*. He tells me to get off if I don't like it, that I can walk back on my own. I slide down and burn the side of my calf on the exhaust pipe, then step back to see if Mom is getting off with me. She is saying something, her lips making shapes with nothing coming out because there aren't any other sounds besides the sound of the motor. Gary looks like he's having the time of his life as he turns them toward the end of the road and speeds off, all the way past where the road bends, and then farther, toward the highway and wherever else.

I walk back home alone, keeping my eyes on the dirt in front of me while my bones shake like I'm still there on the back of the motorcycle and no one is ever going to let me off.

Up on the step stool to brush my teeth, I open wide and each one is still there, white and sharp. I count them starting at the back, feel them with my fingers to make double-sure they're not going to fall out. Gary took off for a few days and Mom seems resigned to it, not glad and not upset either. At night she puts her Milton record on and hums along, singing the lyrics. I have a deep cut across my forehead, and Mom says no school until it heals up a bit. A week with no Mr. Kohl, and Toby having to cover for me with whatever excuse Mom uses when she calls the school secretary. Mom says I need to do better at reading Gary's signs, to hide away when Gary gets too high, which is different than when he is just drunk.

"How can you tell he's getting dangerous?" she asks me, a pop quiz.

"Shiny eyes and his jaw starts clenching," I say.

"Good," she says, "What else?"

"You start getting nicer to him," I say.

She picks at a hangnail on her thumb and pushes her hair out of her eyes, wraps it behind her ear but it doesn't stay.

"I guess that's true," she says.

She says he didn't mean to cut me on purpose, I was just there when he got mad and threw that beer can, still half full. That's why she is quizzing me on the warning signs.

Mom herself is wearing two black eyes, pop, pop—Raccoon

Mom, Lone Ranger Mom—and her old bathrobe that's starting to unravel at the bottom.

"I think he could still be a good man, we just have to try harder when he comes back," she says and none of it makes sense, both of us busted up together but alone.

The music tries to lift the hard feelings off us, tries to move them up and out, through the window and into the wind that's blowing outside, out past the rooftops and the fields and gone, but Milton is not enough.

"Even when I want to," she says as the needle gets to the end of the record, "I don't know how I could ever get rid of him—I don't know how I could get him to go away for good."

Mom isn't feeling well, says all those Lucky Strikes are catching up with her, and I better not ever pick up this terrible habit, that nicotine is like tar in your lungs, black tar that sticks and burns. I've already got my own tar, but she doesn't know that. She coughs into her sleeve and makes more tea, says she's just glad it's Saturday at least and she doesn't have to miss any work—that she can't miss any shifts because bills are piling up.

Gary left for work earlier. He has a weekend job at a gas station now, filling up people's tanks and selling corn nuts and licorice ropes and beef jerky. I heard him slam the front door as he left, tripping down the porch steps, the jarring metal whir of engine and radio sending their waves all the way in through my closet door. Last night I couldn't sleep, stayed awake in the dark with my stomach knives, worried about when my period will come like Mom said, worried that's what this pain is about because I haven't figured out how to turn into a boy who won't get one.

"Go out and play a bit," Mom says, rubbing her temples, and feeling the front sides of her neck for swollen glands.

It feels too early to go outside, too cold with the dampness heavy all around us, dripping from the fig tree, from the rotten sunflower stalks, from the old clothesline.

"Can't I just stay here with you?" I ask, and she looks at me like I am a stranger to her. Our view of each other across the living room feels far away—peering at each other through the furniture from a great distance with more clarity. I'm not sure if I recognize her either. On her face, the shallows of her cheeks are slowly sinking into a cavern of their own making, like beige quicksand, like sinkholes, like traps. Even her hair is dull, not the usual shiny, dark mane but a different color, not gray exactly, but a new shade of lifelessness.

"Go outside, Smokes," she says again, more sternly than the last time, before another coughing fit. "I just need to be alone for a little bit. Go for a little walk and count how many birds you recognize. Come back and tell me all their names."

"Why aren't I enough for you?" I ask, but I'm looking down at the floor when I say it, and she doesn't hear. She's blowing her nose and pulling a thin blanket around her shoulders. Her eyes have gray rings underneath them, heavy with sleep.

I go to the door, put on a jacket over my pajamas and pull on a knit cap, slide my feet into rain boots. Moonshadow peeks out from under the couch and blinks.

Outside it's not as cold as I thought it would be, no frost on the ground, just clear air that smells like rain. The sun is coming up over the rounded hills in the distance. I know Mom said to count birds, but the cold reaches down my neck when I lift my head up to the limbs or the sky. Instead, I count every stick and leaf I step over, keeping a tally: fourteen broken sticks, thirty-seven yellow leaves. By the time I get to Old Oak, I'm up to ninety sticks and two hundred leaves. I count spider webs, too, only four of them, catching the light and glistening like tinsel. The black spiders spin their threads, and I step around and over and under, trying not to ruin their work. I count freckles on my arms, I count mushrooms. These ones are small and white, with little hairs at their necks. They are little forest people with hats that are too big. They've just been born, emerging from the muck and looking around, astonished by their own little bodies, soft and shiny. I pick up a stick and draw a circle in the mud where they stand looking up at me—draw it over and over until the shape holds its form, keeping the water from seeping in and erasing it. I poke in two black holes for eyes and set acorns there, making a slash for a small mouth. I pick up two brown leaves for the ears and add some neon green lichen for hair. I have made my own head in case Mom never gets around to it, in case she keeps sinking into herself until she dissolves, in case Gary breaks the painting where my flat body lives and the last of me disappears. I realize if Mom dissolves there will be no one left to remember who we were.

Some sun peeks through the trees and warms my left cheek where it lands, but I stuff my hands in my pockets because the air is still cool around me. I lay down so my neck lines up with the head I've crafted. I'm careful not to hurt the little mushroom family who is watching me, alive and sturdy with their above-ground bodies at last. I feel the wet earth seep into my legs and arms and my head rests heavy on its own image. I keep my eyes closed for one minute, then five, take deep breaths, pretend I'm a fallen tree, I'm a tired goose, I'm a salamander glowing orange, I'm a long, yellow slug spinning silver from my tailbone, I'm a dead body and I'll never move again, never open my eyes and never say another thing.

"Goodbye," I want to say, but my lips won't move—there's no more voice left.

Cold, cold, cold, and I can feel the weight of myself slowly sinking back into the darker place the mushrooms came from. When I do open my eyes, I am counting again—how many leaves are left on the maple tree, how many acorns have yet to fall—and the birds, the ones Mom wanted me to count and name. Two slender sparrows flit through the branches and four juncos are busy with their errands. There are seven crows today, Mom's favorite. Mom said once that the number seven is lucky, that when that number presents itself to you—even if it feels impossible—it's a sign that something is finally going to go right.

Mom says she is feeling better, says the fever burned away a bunch of crud, but when she says it she winces because her lips are still bruised and puffy from Gary's touch. She talks as though I can't actually see her face, as if I don't know the truth.

"That's what fevers are for," she continues, "they blaze through infections and leave the rest of you to heal."

My green army backpack is stuffed with my sleeping bag, warm clothes, a toothbrush, dried fruit, and a couple cans of beans. Mom's carrying everything else, including Moonshadow in an old, rusty cat carrier filled with hay and fresh greens. Without saying it out loud, neither of us wanted to leave him with Gary.

"We're getting out of here," Mom had told me earlier in the morning, looking bright in the face, her eyes dancing before me. "We're going to Little Frog Lake."

I've heard her talk about this place, east of us, in the Cascade Mountains. She went up there a few times when she was younger, when she had a boyfriend who loved the outdoors. He taught her how to start a fire for cooking, how to stay warm in a windstorm. I asked her what happened to him but she pretended she didn't hear me and rummaged through the drawers for a plastic bag.

"You'll love it there," she said, changing the subject, and told me to go find batteries for the flashlight.

Gary wasn't home as we packed up the car. His white van was gone from where it usually sat along the curb, but all his clothes were still on the floor in Mom's room, so I knew he'd be coming back.

Yesterday, Mom spent the afternoon on the couch with a bag of frozen lima beans on her eye, a bag of frozen peas on her bottom lip, and a bag of frozen tater tots on her right shoulder. After her face got numb, she asked me to pump first aid spray onto her cuts as she closed her eyes and explained how antibiotics work, how with my help she'll heal up quick.

We lock up the house and head east on the highway. Bob Dylan is on the radio and Mom hums along, taps her fingers on the steering wheel. Her profile is back to her crow-self, wild. Her lips are puffy and discolored despite the ice, and the cut above her left eye has a bump that she says throbs in time to the lyrics: *Don't think twice it's alright.*

"We should've brought the frozen peas," I say.

She turns her eyes away from the road to look at me and says Little Frog Lake is full of magic and special healing powers, and it is exactly what we both need.

We pass the abandoned Gingerbread House Diner on the side of the road where the mountains start getting steep and get coffee and hot chocolate at the gas station, buy extra water jugs, and a postcard of two spotted owls sitting in a tree near Opal Lake. Mom tells me that spotted owls are monogamous and stay in the same pair for life, roam around the forest all year and then come back to the very same nest. Mom is not an owl then, but maybe another kind of bird, like the wild turkey who doesn't fall in love, just goes where it wants, gobbling and scratching and running for cover between the trees. Wild turkeys are tough, even with their long, elegant necks.

When we get to the trailhead parking lot, I fill up Moonshadow's water bottle and put on a second jacket. It's late afternoon already and the air is colder than in town. The tree branches shimmer from the afternoon's rain. The red cedar trees on the trail to the lake are even taller than Old Oak and my lungs burn with each step—the cold mountain air scouring me from the inside. The pine trees sway like dancers and drop their needles to the damp ground. Next to us, the creek is full and rushing over heavy rocks dark with moss.

Mom says it's two miles uphill, but we have the creek to keep us company, and in its gurgles are voices so clear it sounds like people are talking in an old language. But there are no people— we are the only ones here, because though the snow has melted, it is still wet and dark. Mom says most people prefer to go into the woods when it's summer—this way we have it all to ourselves. Even though she is tired, from Gary, from the backpack, from carrying Moonshadow, and from me, she is still alive and strong and leading us somewhere special.

She doesn't say much. She keeps her feet moving and points out different plants. There are sword ferns as big as me, and when we stop for a snack, we crouch down low and she tells me to imagine we are only a few inches tall and how vast the world would feel if it were true. She stops in a clearing and points up to a raven, explaining how they are different from the crows at home. It watches us from the low branch of a young hemlock, cocking its head to the side and listening to our human mumblings. I ask her how she learned so much about all the trees and animals, and she says she was born in Moss River and never escaped, so decided to learn the names of all the plants and animals who never escaped either.

Now that I've been here, Deer and I will definitely be able to find it again.

It is past dinner-time when we get to the lake, and the low clouds sag, heavy with darkness. The still lake water glimmers in blues and grays and silvers. We put up our tent and set up our sleeping bags on mats, make pillows out of our extra clothes. Mom asks me to find short sticks and branches and helps me put leaves and pine needles at the bottom of the fire circle. She flicks her lighter and the whole thing goes up in a whoosh despite the moisture, all crackling warmth like magic. She heats up a can of chili and tears off hunks of bread, and we sit on fallen trees eating the best dinner we've ever had. Around us, the sky grows even darker with no moon, only clouds. My stomach knives are put away for now and I look up—there's Mom's tired face glowing orange in the light as she pulls her jacket tighter around her skinny shoulders. Her split lip still has a line of dried blood but is already less swollen, and all her visible bruises are fading to a golden yellow. For a moment she's forgotten I'm there, but then looks down and smiles.

"Tomorrow we will do a polar bear jump in the lake," she says, and I picture our bodies covered with thick white fur, all muscle and weight, with the smell of fresh fish on our breath.

She adds some wood to the fire, and I lean against her. Her arms wrap around my shoulders, and she pulls me in tight. Above us, an owl calls to another owl and their sounds echo back and forth in song.

"There are people called the Babemba," she tells me as the fire crackles and sends up signals. "They live in South Africa and when someone does something terrible, something thought to be unforgivable, they don't send that person to jail or kick them out to be homeless or do anything punishing at all. What they do is have the person stand in the middle of the village, and one by one, everyone says something positive that person has done, a contribution they've made. The person who messed up has to listen to their love and forgiveness until they can let it in and start to heal."

Her arm is around me and the warm firelight flickers against my face. I'm worried she knows everything about my dirt-eating, about hiding my stomach knives, about wanting Gary gone, and all the hatred I feel, having to flush twice so Mom doesn't know my blood is coming out more than before—all the darkness inside me building up and spilling over. Maybe I'm supposed to stand here and wait for her kindness to love me back to life.

Or maybe it's Mom who wants to be forgiven, for not paying attention, for not making my stomach better, for not loving me enough to have it be the two of us. Maybe she's putting herself into the circle and is waiting for me to tell her all the positive things. But then, though our regular life is very far away, a sinking realization takes hold of my ribcage—the person she is talking about is Gary—and when we get home he will be there, unpredictable and cruel, but Mom will keep trying to love him back to being his best and truest self.

We climb into our sleeping bags as the fire dies out, and Mom's breathing gets slow and even just like it did back in my closet. Moonshadow scratches out a nest made of douglas fir branches and moss I collected and placed in the back of our tent so he can feel like a wild rabbit at least for one night. My legs are heavy weights now, holding me down so surely to this place, and I want to stay here forever, to never go back to Moss River, to never go home. Moonshadow and I will set up life in these mountains and Deer will come to find us; I'll even let my hair grow long, eat fern fronds, and spend my morning gathering pine needles that Mom said have lots of vitamin C if you make a tea out of them. I'll camp on the banks of this lake until Mom realizes that Gary isn't going to let himself be forgiven and kicks him out and changes the locks, or until Gary gets caught violating his parole, or someone catches him hurting us, or until he steals again or gets pulled over driving drunk or high or whatever else he might do to break this bad bond.

In the morning Mom lets me make the fire by myself, says it's something she can teach me that I'll use my whole life, and that when I'm old, sitting in the warmth of one I made myself, to remember this one thing she did right. I gather up the pine twigs, some bigger sticks, and a bigger part of a log that rotted off. She says to build it up strong so it's burning extra hot when we come back from jumping in the lake.

The clouds have cleared for now, and at the edge of the water the sun is coming up above the tallest trees and steam rises from our mouths. We strip down to bare skin and Mom's bruises pulse in the light in the same colors of the sunrise—purple, green, and yellow on her hips, legs, and back—but this cold water might wash them away, make us both healed and new, make us into different people with this forest spell.

Naked and shivering, Mom says the best way is to run as fast as we can and jump, that slowly wading in is a kind of torture. I remember my night alone under the bridge, racing past the troll, and how scared I felt, but also how brave and ready. We hold hands and count to three, running until we let go of each other and are under all that sharp cold, the trees cheering us on, the clear water cleaning us like nothing else ever has. Mom lets out an animal shriek and laughs when her head comes up, and I take a picture with my mind of her smile and brilliance, framed by dark green trees and the silvery water holding us as if we've always belonged here in this forest—it just took us a while to figure it out.

"Let's stay here forever, Smokey," Mom says.

We are by the fire, drying off. My skin is humming with electricity and even though I'm shaking, I want to jump in again and again.

"You look so alive," Mom says, and pulls me into her body to warm me up. "Don't forget how alive you are," she says, and I promise her I won't.

When we pull up into the driveway, Gary is on the porch smoking, and I can't tell if he is happy or angry to have us back, but it doesn't matter because Bingo is there with him, sitting on the steps—not even on a leash—like he's lived with us his whole life.

"We got ourselves a dog," he says, and I can't imagine how it happened—good things don't come this easily. The magic from the lake hasn't worn off yet.

I keep out of reach of Gary and walk toward Bingo with my hand out. When I reach him, he yawns and licks my palm, wags his tail.

"He's so skinny," Mom says, grabbing Moonshadow and her backpack out of the car, walking toward Gary with the same caution I did—she's not sure anymore what Gary has in store for her.

When she gets to him, he pulls her onto his lap, and asks how camping was, but doesn't wait for an answer. He shoves his tongue into Mom's mouth, and I walk past them, but Gary shoots out his arm and grabs my leg.

"That piece of shit Edwin from down the street is gone," he says. "Foxy is in the hospital now and Edwin's in jail. That asshole raped her almost to death. Cops were swarming the neighborhood yesterday. I guess Hank found her by the sidewalk under some bushes when he left for work. Edwin's turned eighteen, so no juvie for him—he's a goner. Foxy's mom already moved out, didn't even put her things into boxes—shoved some clothes and a lamp into her car, and drove away—probably didn't remember Bingo was still tied up in the back. Doubt she wanted him anyway—he was Edwin's dog."

Gary tells us this like it's no big deal, like hearing a story on the news—he doesn't feel sad that the person this happened to is just a girl who wears bright pink jeans and has a sweater with a unicorn on it. Nothing gets to Gary—he never floats up, just takes up all the room around him with his wide, mean body, only wanting things for himself.

"Doesn't Foxy go to your school?" he asks.

He has a smile on his face, but then it changes and his lips go back to being thin, straight lines.

I tell him she is supposed to be in fifth grade this year but hasn't been showing up much, and he nods as if something makes sense.

Mom looks at me, wants to know how I'm reacting to all this news. It's as if she can hear my stomach knives starting to slice, but our closeness from the lake is fading already. Even though she wants to hug me and make sure I'm okay, and even though I want her to wrap her arms around me, neither of us moves now, because Gary is a thick wall that keeps us separated.

I float up and there's Foxy and her small body—there's Edwin's big body, too, smothering hers with his weight. I want to ask Foxy if she yelled or stayed quiet, if she thought someone might help her, or if she knew no one was coming. I hope she floated up so she didn't have to feel everything. I want to ask if she was found with clothes on or naked, if she had bruises like Mom. I want to walk the hospital halls and find out who is with her there. Who will she be now? How will people treat her now that this thing has happened and will always have happened?

I float up higher, where the air is thinner and cooler, but then a sudden warmth brings me back down in an instant, like

I'm not a ghost at all—instead, I'm a smooth stone and fall down through the sky to remember that Bingo is with us now. He licks my hand to remind me.

Bingo tilts his head and gives me a nod, saying he got my messages about trying to help him. Heading inside, I pick up Moonshadow in his box where Mom left him, and Bingo leaves Gary and Mom behind without a second thought. He follows right on my heels to make sure I understand that he has been waiting for me and is glad I'm home.

In the living room, I put down Moonshadow's box and eye Bingo.

"You two are going to need to be friends," I tell them.

Moonshadow gives a scratch on the floor of his box and Bingo takes a sniff, wags his tail, and then starts exploring the rest of the house. I take him on a tour.

"This is the bathroom, this is the living room, this is the kitchen. Don't ever go into Mom's room. Here is our closet."

I get him a bowl of water and set Moonshadow on my lap. Bingo comes close and Moonshadow's heart beats fast, his whiskers tremble, but Bingo has no interest. He laps up water and asks what's for dinner.

I think about Mom's plan to love Gary back to himself like the Babemba. Through the window, Gary keeps grabbing Mom like he's playing a fun game, but he's being too rough, and she's pretending she likes it. I want to be back at the clean, cold lake, but at least Bingo is here now.

Bingo and Moonshadow and I go and sit in my closet, and Toby calls on the walkie-talkie, asks if I heard what happened.

"Bet she's gonna have a baby now," he says and my stomach knives clank around, not sure what to do with themselves. "Wanna meet me?" he asks.

Mom and Gary are in the bedroom now and I walk right out the door without even having to be extra quiet because no one will hear me anyways. We meet at Old Oak, and it's getting dark. Bingo runs back and forth across the trail, sniffing everything, smelling all this new freedom.

Toby is as excited about Bingo being saved as I am—he practically bounces off his heels in his enthusiasm. Bingo runs around, cocking his head when voices and easy laughter from the camp sound out in the dusk—someone is having a party.

"I hope no one gets raped down there," Toby says, squinting across the field as someone turns on a radio to Q105.

Bingo sits next to us listening to the muffled beats of the radio's Top 40, his mottled coat blending in with all the browns and grays around us as light falls. He leans in close enough that I can feel his body heat.

"Gary might be a rapist," I tell Toby, and he looks down at the dirt.

"Hanky-Panky might be one, too," he says, his voice low.

He stands up, pulls his wool hat down snug over his ears as he takes a deep breath, faces back toward our houses, and yells louder than I've ever heard him: "GO AWAY, YOU GODDAMN RAPISTS!" over and over until I get up, too, and yell along with him.

Bingo tucks his tail at first, then starts running all over in a frenzy. We are yelling to the trees and the air and the neighborhood beyond this patch of wild land. We are yelling at the Edwins and Garys and Hanks and Richards and all the others, yelling until our voices go dry and quiet. When Toby's voice cracks, he leans against the tree, breathing hard as if he just ran around the school track, as my own ears ring in the silence that follows.

Toby says he has to go home, or he'll get in trouble, and gets up to leave—no bouncing heels now, but a weight has lifted off him. He turns onto the path with his serious face and his hands in his pockets. I pick up a sharp stick, draw symbols in the dirt, and watch him go. His pants are not long enough to cover his ankles anymore, flooding out at the bottom, snagging branches as he makes his way up the deer trail and out of sight.

Bingo wore himself out, not used to so much running. He's panting on the wet ground, stretching out long. Old Oak is shimmering in the dusk, looking bare and dead, but near the top are the slimmest of green leaves emerging. Deer won't come now with this new, strange creature by my side, not until I find a way to convince her that he is gentle, not even interested in harming a small black rabbit. I nibble on a dead leaf and taste the rich wetness of it.

In school last week, Mr. Kohl taught us about the Native Americans as if they're all dead, but Kaleb is still out there somewhere, not too far away. It helps me to remember that he is not too far off. I wanted to tell Mr. Kohl how wrong he was, but also didn't want to explain Kaleb to him—doing so might break the spell of a good memory I want to keep to myself.

"You and Kaleb would have been friends," I say to Bingo. "Amos would have liked you, too."

I don't want to go home too early and hear more of Mom and Gary's animal noises—I want to be here by my tree—warm enough and alive enough. I sink down next to Bingo in the damp and he puts his tired head in my lap. I pet his soft ears and tell him over and over again how glad I am he got free, that I'll take care of him, and that everything is going to be better from now on. He sighs a big sigh in the hope it's all true while above us the first stars of the evening shine out from in between gaps in the clouds. The radio music down below fades out into the sound of frogs croaking into the coolness of this dark Oregon night.

The Art House downtown shows mostly foreign films, and Mom starts taking me now that I am almost nine and can sit still and read the subtitles when necessary. She says Gary prefers superhero movies and rolls her eyes. We've sat in the dark before, watching *Jesus of Montreal*, *Do the Right Thing*, and *My Life as a Dog*. My stomach still aches remembering Sputnik out there alone in outer space.

The red walls of the theater slope down to concessions with old movie posters lining the hallway and classical music playing behind the register. Mom gets black coffee and we share a striped bag of popcorn with extra butter. The woman who owns the one-room theater is named Maggie and has kind eyes and curly bleached hair, and sometimes I pretend she is Great-Aunt Josephine and that she'll start taking care of me when Mom goes out and leaves me at home alone. She always beams at me when I come in and tells Mom how impressed she is that someone my age can sit still and read all the subtitles.

"You make my kids seem like Neanderthals," she says, laughing to herself as she gets our popcorn ready, her necklaces jangling as she pumps out the butter.

Maggie gives me a wink as she gives Mom her change.

"This movie is supposed to be excellent," Mom says as we find some seats near the front. There are three other people in the theater, two older women and an old man all sitting together like pigeons in their gray outfits. "I love matinees," Mom says, "We almost have the whole place to ourselves."

My Beautiful Laundrette starts and here are Johnny and Omar, flirting amongst the thugs and kissing in the back room of the laundrette. I look at Mom out of the corner of my eye, wanting to understand her opinion of these young men, but her face reveals nothing. I wonder if she might let me change my name now, not to Rocky, but to Johnny—and let me bleach my hair and wear tight work caps when I leave the house for school. Or I could be an Omar and slip my lean body into fitted suits and pay people in cash and beam out an easy smile even when it seems like nothing is going to work out. I think of David in New York, if he really made it all the way there, and if this is what he found.

I wonder if Mom has ever had any friends like these men who kiss each other and wouldn't want her in the way she likes to be wanted. There are two women in town who Mom explained to me are lesbians, but she isn't friends with them either. They own a cafe that Mom took me to as a treat after my booster shot. Right after the shot, my face streaked with tears, I told her and the nurse that I would kill myself if I ever had to get another booster, and they both leaned toward me with concern.

"What do you mean?" Mom asked, as she and the nurse exchanged worried glances.

I knew it was an alarming thing to say, that killing yourself was what people did when they didn't want to keep going through things. It was what Toby meant when he fake blew his brains out in the driveway, and I remember Mom once yelling she wished I was dead, wished that I'd never been born at all. These were some of the different kinds of endings. Later she apologized and said she didn't mean any of it. I don't want to hurt myself, but to not exist sometimes sounds a lot easier than to keep on going. Toby agreed with me when I explained it to him, and I wonder if we are the only kids who think like this.

The booster shot wasn't even that terrible, but I liked the creases in the nurse's and Mom's faces directed toward me, taut with fear. I considered telling them about my stomach teeth, how they've grown into knives and how they make the toilet bowl red every time I have to poop, that I can't eat very much anymore, that almost everything hurts, and at night now my stomach puffs out like a deflated dodgeball, and I have to sleep on my side and hope it goes flat again by the morning. I thought about telling them that Gary or some other future boyfriend might get around to killing us anyways, so maybe I should just do it myself before they get the chance, but decided to keep that to myself. I could tell I'd already freaked them out enough. Mom took me to the cafe then because she must have thought I needed something special to get my mind off things.

At the café, the lesbians were cheerful. One was short and the other was tall; they both had dark brown hair and one wore a cowboy hat. They laughed a lot, smiled at the customers, and joked around. I kept trying to figure out what part of them made them lesbian, tried to know how they were that one thing—they just seemed happy. When we sat down at a little table in the window, I asked Mom what lesbians were, and Mom said they were women who fell in love with each other and had sex, too—that they didn't need men for any of it. The hairs on the back of my neck stood up and I wanted to ask her a lot more questions. But the way she was looking at me—carefully paying attention to what I might say or do next—made me stay quiet.

Last year I found a magazine shoved behind some bushes near the school, and in it there were lots of naked men with huge dicks with bulging veins that looked like dirty rivers, and there were naked women on boats, naked women on beaches, and sometimes there were two naked women and one naked man and they were all doing the thing that Mom later explained was sex.

"But what you saw in that magazine wasn't *really* sex," she says, confusing me. "All you need to know right now is that everyone who is doing it should want to be doing it, and it should never involve children."

This makes sense and doesn't make sense. When I think about White Richard I get the same sick feeling as when I hear Mom and Gary in bed, or when Toby tells me certain things.

Lately, Toby can't stop talking about Edwin and his penis, can't talk about anything else except penises. He says when Edwin goes to prison someone should make him wear under-wear made out of wires that will never let the penis come out, so he can't hurt anyone else, and if his penis tries to escape, the wires will electrocute his dick to oblivion. Toby can still talk for hours about how Mr. Kohl keeps getting hard-ons in class— has talked about it for months now like it's his favorite subject. Sometimes during reading, I look at Toby and his book isn't even turned around the right way because he's staring at Mr. Kohl's crotch, vigilant as a hawk. I'm not sure if Toby would like *My Beautiful Laundrette* or not but maybe something would make sense if he could sit in the dark and watch these young men and their happiness, that maybe being a grown-up man doesn't have to be the worst thing that could happen.

Even when we get on the walkie-talkies, it's just more of a chance for Toby to talk about penises and the men they belong to, and how maybe he's not a man or doesn't have to be a man— he doesn't want to grow up to be a Mr. Kohl or a Hanky-Panky, but what else can he be? He doesn't say all this so clearly, but he eyes everyone around him, studying their dicks and trying to make decisions about what kind of man each one is, and who can be trusted and who can't.

Kaleb might be the only good one left. I bet he's found another kid to give him rental carpet massages and has forgot-ten about me. If he ever does remembers me, I hope he wishes he'd never left. I will try to remember to tell Toby about Kaleb so Toby can believe kind men exist and can try to grow up to be one of those. I'll tell him about Amos, too, locked up for no good reason and missing his dog. I'll tell Toby that maybe he doesn't even have to be a human man when he grows up, he can grow up to be like Deer instead, not with antlers and hooves but in the quiet way Deer waits and listens, the way she nibbles so seriously, and her nimbleness—kind of like Toby already is with his tippy-toe walk and how he notices everything.

The last time we were at Old Oak together, we heard three gunshots and jumped as the birds scattered.

"Who's got a gun?" he asked me.

"Who got shot?" I asked at the same time.

Neither of us said anything else.

We walked back toward our houses, looking for a dead body and not wanting to find it. Maybe Gary finally decided to make Moonshadow into a meal—but he wouldn't have needed a gun for that.

"Maybe Hanky shot himself," Toby said.

"Or maybe Hanky shot Gary."

We walked in silence, nothing but the sound of sticks snapping beneath our feet and birds chatting in the trees. We kept wondering which of the men we know might have shot the gun and who he might have shot. We worried about our moms with their bruises and their need, and their decisions that had led us to this place where these men and their metal are invited in so easily.

The movie ends and I look over at Mom's face, her beautiful bird beak, her eyes straight ahead and focused because she's still in that other world. Her body is looser and lighter, held by the red velvet seats. I want to ask what movie is coming out next and if she'll keep taking me with her so we can sit close together in the dark with so many questions passing over me as the blue screen flickers against my skin and calls on me to pay attention.

Travis is a little older than me, the same grade as Foxy, and he skateboards behind the school every chance he can get. His mom promised him if he finishes this school year, he can drop out to become a professional skateboarder, and now all he does is count the weeks. He decorated a t-shirt with a sharpie to read *Moss River Sucks!* He hates this town. We all do. We can feel it more strongly than the adults—that this is a place closing in on itself, sinking down into a deep hole of its own making.

Travis is a legend all the way down to the first-graders. He wears fingerless gloves and a red leather jacket, same as his hero Michael Jackson. I work hard to get the "Thriller" video and Gary out of my head. Last year, Travis won first place at a skate contest in Portland, and at the school assembly, the principal made him come up on stage to get a high-five. At lunch, Travis was showing off the bus ticket his mom got him to go to L.A. with his older brothers to compete down there.

"It's not fair," says Toby when I tell him. He has a look in his eyes like he's going to kill someone if he can't find a way to get on that bus, too—not to L.A., but to anywhere else. He rubs his sneaker in the dirt, and I think he's either going to punch something or run away. Toby says he can't tell what size Travis's dick is but that he saw Hanky-Panky's little dick again last night when he came out of the shower with no towel. When he saw Toby watching him, he grabbed it and wagged it around until Toby ran to his room.

"Penises are disgusting," Toby concludes and starts telling me about how you can tell how big someone's penis is by how big their nose is but then stops talking because Travis's skateboard rolls by us and Travis comes running after it, yelling back to his friends about if they saw him jump over the curb higher than the last time.

Mom got me a plastic board with cheap wheels from Kmart that doesn't roll or bend right and is hard to turn, but I've started bringing it to school, wanting to be part of this. The teachers never go to the empty parking lot across the street from the school so that's where kids go to do their skateboarding tricks, with no one to get angry and threaten to call home. I weave between Travis and his friends, who laugh at jokes I don't understand. They nod and give high-fives over various things they say under their breath, and one of them asks Travis why he lets babies hang around now. He shrugs and says something that makes them shut up. Toby is upset because I haven't been sitting with him as much, but sometimes he watches us skate around anyway, looking more alone than ever as the cannery smoke-stack sends up its gray fumes.

After school, Travis lets me help him set up a course to weave in and out of for practice. I try to go through, to keep up—try not to fall where the cement gets bumpy. When I look up, Travis's not behind me as I thought, but off to the side, still and watching. He comes over to me, his shove unexpected, and I fall backward onto my elbows, ripping open the fabric of my jacket at the armpit. He comes at me again, pulls me up, grabs my jacket, and shoves me against the back wall. He's about to punch me in the stomach or slam me hard but then he leans down and presses his cold, wet mouth against mine, and his dirty fingers rub around my crotch through my jeans. His face doesn't show any feelings and his lips are hard. The knives slice but something else rises, too: a warm electricity.

"You kiss like a fucking boy," he tells me when he is done, then gives me one final shove backward against the wall and watches me—his taut face smeared with disappointment now.

I wonder how he knows this—maybe he has his own White Richard or has kissed boys in his grade, or other younger kids like me. There are sixth-graders who call him a faggot in the halls, but I thought it was because he has long hair and listens to Depeche Mode too loud on his Walkman.

"You kiss like a boy," he says again, but I didn't think I had kissed him at all.

I flash to Foxy, who no one in our neighborhood has heard from since what happened.

"You better not tell anyone about this," Travis says, close enough that I could lick the stray eyelash off his cheek.

My stomach knives are strangely still. Their gleaming blades wait together in a line, looking for a sign. I wipe off my mouth, step away from Travis, and pick up my skateboard. He sits down on the ground and punches his own leg over and over, a dull boy drum. He is not looking at me anymore—he's somewhere else— at a skate competition far away. I walk, then run toward home, don't look back. Two blocks from our house I throw up on the sidewalk, bits of dark stuff thick with red.

I wonder what Tyler, Alex, and Lisa are doing right then, imagine them at home eating a snack that one of their moms made, something warm and sweet. They are in clean clothes on a white couch, watching something funny on TV. They're together and happy and far away—even though probably just a few streets over from this puddle of vomit below me.

At home, I want to cry but can't. I lie on the couch because Mom and Gary aren't home, so there's no one to tell me to go to my closet and leave them alone. I let Bingo lick my entire face clean. He tells me not to worry, that everyone has a bad day sometimes.

I get up and run a bath like Mom does for me, shoving my ripped jacket underneath my mattress. The hot water stings my elbows, stings my palms, and stings everything else, while I use the washcloth to rub away the skin where Travis's fingers prodded. I dip my head under, paw my shorn head, and blow bubbles to the top like a sea creature.

Dried off and in my closet, I call Toby on the walkie-talkie, not sure how much to explain.

"Travis messed with me," I say, not telling him about the secret warmth—I won't tell anyone that part.

Over, over.

"Everyone says he's a pedo," Toby tells me through the static, and my silence must tell him I'm lost because he explains: "Travis is probably going to grow up and have sex with little kids. Over."

All the knives that live in my stomach started slicing, and back in the bathroom, I sit over the toilet and have to flush twice to make sure Mom won't see my blood coming out more than ever before.

All of it comes to me at that moment, one minute sitting alone with these old feelings and this new word explained, and the next moment floating up so fast like a taut balloon, away from my sore body, away from Toby explaining that it's regular kids who can turn into monsters, up to the top of our house, but it isn't daylight anymore—everything is black.

I am back in the bathroom with White Richard, before Mom gets home and pounds on the door to save me. The tiles are faded white with cracked grout between each one. The curtains are ones Mom sewed from an old sheet—pale blue with small, yellow flowers, fraying at the hems. The bathtub faucet drips, drips, drips—just one small leak, but the porcelain is stained darker where the water hits. White Richard has one of his meaty hands holding me still. He uses the weight of that arm to keep me right there before him so I can't float away, can't escape out through the window and up and gone to be with the plants and animals outside. With his other hand, knuckles calloused and scarred, he is pulling off my superhero underwear, the ones with Spiderman throwing out a web that I begged Mom to get me. He leans down closer, and I see dark hairs sprouting from his chin, his gray, cracked lips, and I can smell him. Old meat. Old onions. Now he is at the V of my legs with his cold, mean mouth saying, *You like it, don't tell anyone, You like it, don't tell anyone.*

Over and over—it will never stop.

There's a sound outside, a shrill bird calling out for help. It's a blue jay on the branch outside the bathroom window. He scrapes his beak on the branch like sharpening a dull knife, looks in the window and squawks again: *Noooo, Nooo, Nooo.*

White Richard moves his hand over my mouth even though I'm dead silent, trying not to breathe even—I am willing Mom to come home and stop this. I'm willing the bird to fly to Old Oak and not tell anyone what he saw. I don't want the animals to know this is possible, this feeling that is so much worse than any other. I'm crying but with no sound, just two warm, salty creeks streaking down. I know that I don't exist to White Richard—I'm not a real person at all.

Do I exist? I ask the walls, because the bird couldn't keep listening and flew away. I can't hear any kind of answer over the sound of White Richard's ragged breathing. I look down and his penis has slithered part of the way out of his jeans. It's dark pink and alive and he knows I've looked. He smiles a wide smile, and says, *It's so big now.* He takes it all the way out. It is throbbing as if it has its own heartbeat, its own mind, and he rubs it all over my stomach and up to my lips and then down to where I'm cold and wet from his mean mouth between my legs. His breathing gets louder and louder and my tears have all dried up. He gasps like he's dying and then Mom is banging on the cheap, plywood door.

Over, over.

Mom is home now, and the White Richard from all those years ago is gone, too, disappeared like a ghost back into my memories.

Mom is shaking me saying, "Wake up, wake up! Baby, are you okay?"

I stand up too quickly, coughing up an acidic sickness, and the world spins around me. Mom is so worried, trying to figure something out. She pulls me close into her chest, and her neck smells like lavender soap and sweat. Again and again, she asks me what happened, but I don't want to talk about White Richard's ghost, don't want to risk bringing him back again.

I ask to stay in bed with Bingo and Moonshadow curled up near me, these creatures who won't ask me to explain anything, no matter what happened or what will happen next. These peaceful animals know how to get along. Mom makes me chamomile tea with honey and sits next to me in the closet, pulling me in to lean against her. The walkie-talkie is mostly static now. The batteries are running low. Mom rubs my back like she won't ever stop as I drift off into an exhausted, dark dream of nothingness.

Gary came home late last night, and I was already asleep in bed, too tired to keep watch. This morning he comes out of Mom's bedroom wearing black and blue all over his big swollen cheeks. He can't open his mouth because he has a jaw brace holding his teeth closed. Mom says *poor baby* and pets the back of his head like he's an injured mountain lion, claws half pulled back.

He can't yell at us for now and I start to think we got lucky, but then—his arms and legs and feet still work, and his scabby fist is clenching and unclenching to a strange rhythm.

Mom says he'll have to eat everything through a straw for at least a month, maybe longer. She says for breakfast it'll be scrambled eggs in the blender, and for dinner, hamburger and mashed potatoes the same way.

Mom doesn't have regular friends, only boyfriends. She used to talk to her old friend Angela but doesn't anymore, says Angela can't be trusted, that she's a conniving bitch she wishes she'd never met. Cherry and Mom aren't friends either, but sometimes they wave to each other from across the road, a half-hearted wave, neither wanting to get too close—two wary coyotes, keeping a safe distance.

As we drive by Toby's house, Mom and I keep our eyes straight ahead, not wanting to attract attention—Hanky-Panky is in the yard yelling about something, looking rabid.

"Hank is a sadist," Mom tells me as we pass their house and pull into the driveway. "Lots of men are sadists. That's why you can't go over there."

Mom and I eat dinner and I don't ask where Gary is, don't say I think Gary is a sadist, too. I try to relax and just be glad he is somewhere else.

"Do you think my dad ever thinks of us? Do you think he wants to come and meet me someday?" I ask.

It comes out before I can figure out if it's the wrong or right thing to talk about.

She looks out the window, and rubs her neck.

"Daniel is not coming for you, babe," she says. "I never told him I was pregnant. I was afraid I'd have to share you, or he would try to take you away from me. And I thought he might not believe that you were his."

I run my finger along my forearm, press the muscle down to the bone, and will myself to be the color of a dark bruise. Mom watches me, then says she needs some alone time and gets up to throw away the pile of cigarette butts collecting in the clay ashtray I made for her in art class.

Outside, the sun is poking out between large, fluffy clouds. The mushroom factory is running, and its thick fumes rise over the treetops to reach us, rank and unavoidable. Disappointment sits heavy on my shoulders, squeezing the back of my neck. This is all there is. No one else is coming for me. Back in my closet, I use my fingernail to scrape some of the yellow off the wall, scratch my true name into the wood. *Rocky Washington. Rocky Washington. Rocky Washington.* I turn on the walkie-talkie, hoping Toby picks up.

"Toby, are you there? Over," I say, not having much hope. Maybe the batteries have finally died, though I can still hear something coming through.

Toby has been talking to me less and less. I've been trying to figure out what I did wrong to make him go away. Mom has been going away more too and I can't make her stay either. When Toby does pick up, at first I'm relieved, ready to see if he wants to go out to the field with me, to get away from our coyote-den houses. Right away though, scared animal fear takes over. Toby is crying and not even trying to pretend he isn't.

I can't understand what he's saying through his tears and wailing and breathing too fast but then he screams in one sick breath, the walkie-talkie clear of static for a last broadcast.

"He's a rapist and a pedo and I couldn't stop him and now I've done this thing."

The way he says it makes me know I need to tell Mom; I can't keep this to myself. In her room, she has a book in her hand, but it's unopened and she's just rubbing her forehead and kind of rocking herself back and forth like she does sometimes when it is all too much. When I tell her about Toby crying, she curses and says she won't get to rest until she's dead, but then she hears the panic in my voice when I tell her what he said. She pulls on her shoes and follows me out the door and across the road. The sky is dark again—the sun has decided to stay behind the clouds forever.

We knock on the door and it opens on its own. Hanky-Panky's car is gone, fresh tracks through the mud where it usually sits. As soon as we step inside my stomach knives shimmer—things are not right. Cherry is on the couch, crumpled like a limp doll tossed out of a car on the side of the freeway. She has cuts on her face slicing across her cheeks, scabs of red and brown. Her right arm is clearly broken—there's more dried blood along her shoulder and her elbow hangs at a disorienting angle, tied up in an old sheet.

There are pill bottles open on the coffee table and an empty bottle of whiskey peeks out from the back cushions of the couch. Ice in a plastic bag is melting onto the floor. Mom goes over to her, but Cherry's eyes are wide and scared. She tries to shake her head no, and then looks with such intensity into the bathroom that we look away from her toward the bathroom, too. That's where we see Toby on the floor, leaning against the doorframe. There's blood on his hands and on his jeans that are pulled halfway down, his face whiter than any face I've ever seen. Mr. Kohl once showed us slides of albino animals and explained the genes, but Toby is whiter than that.

Hanky-Panky must have done something to Toby, maybe stabbed him when he tried to protect Cherry, maybe shot him. There's so much blood, and the knife that Hanky-Panky gave him sits in Toby's right hand. It comes to me in a sick flood that Toby has done this to himself.

"I don't want to be a man, don't want to hurt anyone," Toby says to us, his voice so clear it's an eerie choir of one. I don't understand how he can speak at all. "So I cut it off."

Mom covers her mouth with her hand like she's in the part of a horror movie when the monster first jumps out. She runs back to the other room to look for their phone to call an ambulance. She follows the cord to find it under some old magazine, and punches in 911. Her voice is frantic as she gives the address and answers their questions, says a boy is hurt, says she doesn't know exactly what happened.

My feet are two dead weights cemented into the floor. I look back toward Cherry who is passed out cold now, and her busted-up face has no expression at all, like she's been gone for a long time—not dead, but not alive either. Her red hair is damp with sweat and sticks out in all directions like she's a punk rocker—like she plays the drums in a band in Portland—not like a beaten-up mom with a hurt kid and a bad boyfriend.

I take a step closer to the bathroom, smell cold metal, and can't bring my eyes to where Toby's penis should be because I don't want to know if he did it all the way or not. I don't know what to do or say. Maybe if I was back in my closet with the walkie-talkie I could think of something useful to tell him, but standing here I have nothing to offer. The knife has fallen to the floor with a clank next to Toby's red-wet leg. It catches the flashing light coming through the cracked bathroom window above the toilet as the ambulance finally pulls up outside, screaming its siren screams, scaring away all the nightbirds who gathered on the clothesline to find out what happened.

Mom leaves but doesn't tell me where she's going, just that she'll be back soon. I look for her journal as soon as the door clicks behind her, but it's not in the same place by her bed. I look through her dresser drawers, push around her holey underwear and worn socks, then find it under a stack of books. I don't go back to the beginning like I did before, but to the end, to the last thing she's written.

> *I think Smokey remembered what happened with Richard and I'm afraid Gary could do the same or worse. He is out of his mind right now—wanting his drugs and losing his shit. Even his skin smells like anger, it comes out rancid in his sweat at night. I don't know how to get rid of him. I don't know what he will do if I try. I don't want to be the mother who ends up at the shelter. If I could send Smokey somewhere else I would. I'd do that and handle Gary on my own. Aunt Josephine would know how to help. Gary said if I leave him he'll kill me, kill Smokey, set the house on fire, burn it all to the ground. When he apologizes now I know I can't trust anything he says anymore. I've got to get us away.*

I hear the car pull up, put the journal back where I found it, close the drawers I opened, and go to my closet. I have to help her get us away. I have to figure it out, but I don't know how. When Mom comes in to check on me, I can't look at her because I know I've already let her down.

Gary keeps getting meaner to Mom but still leaves me alone because Bingo growls at him when he comes near me, and Gary always says, *I'll deal with you two later*. It's not hard to understand him, even with his jaw still wired. I tell Bingo to stop growling because Gary might hit him, too, or get rid of him, or worse. Gary's got a gun now. It's silver and heavy. He brought it out to show Mom when she was making dinner and put it in my hand, said I could be a baby bank robber. Mom turned around to see what was going on and went crazy when she saw it.

"Gary, get that fucking gun out of my house," she says and it's the first time I've heard her stand up to Gary, or anyone, so boldly.

She must realize that, too, because she backs up against the refrigerator when he grabs the gun from me and then he holds it under her chin and says *the fucking gun is here to stay*.

Bingo keeps barking at him but nothing else exists to Gary, only him and the gun and Mom. She doesn't take her eyes off Gary but tells me to take Bingo outside and that things will be okay. Nothing is okay. I want to kill Gary, but he will squash me like the spiders he smashes for no reason; he doesn't understand that everyone could get along if he let them.

"Go outside, Smokey," Mom says again in an angry voice, but she's not angry—she is desperate for me to do this thing. "Go outside with Bingo."

Outside, it is raining hard and getting dark. Toby's yard is slick with mud, and it doesn't look like anyone is home. The walkie-talkie is dead. I call him on it anyways, talking into the nothingness.

"S.O.S." I say into the silence, "S.O.S."

I picture him in the hospital, Cherry by his side, maybe praying to God or maybe not. Maybe praying for a better life, out of the mud and away from Hanky-Panky, away from Oregon, out of all this dark wet muck.

In the rain, Bingo shakes off the rain every few steps. He walks a little bit in front of me, leading the way, and looking back at me every few moments to make sure I'm still there. We go past his old house, and he won't look in the yard. He looks straight ahead like it doesn't exist and I decide when I'm older I'll walk by our house and keep my eyes straight ahead, too.

I'm not sure how long I have to stay outside, so I turn back around and cut across our yard, go in through the back door. Bingo shakes off again while I tiptoe to the bathroom for my towel. The house is very quiet and still now. The door to Mom's room is cracked open slightly and I sneak a look, but no one is in there either. It's very dark out now, and the rain is coming down harder. Gary's car is gone, and Mom didn't leave a note. They must have gone out for a drink to cool things off between them, to be around other adults like Mom says she needs. I'm cold and not hungry, and can't imagine ever eating again, but I set out Bingo's dog food and add some warm water because he looks cold, too. I go to my closet and wrap up in all my blankets to try to get warm, but Bingo won't come in after he's done eating. He's sitting alert and upright at the door, looking out like a statue, head cocked and listening. I fall asleep with him silhouetted by the light from the kitchen.

—

This morning the house is still quiet. I'm hungry but scared to eat, afraid the stomach knives will finish me off. I would drink milk to feel better but the carton in the refrigerator has gone sour. The rain has stopped for now, but the ground is still wet and slick. I go out the back door, past the fig tree that is finally starting to brighten again with new, too-early green leaves.

Past the old fence, with Bingo on my heels, fresh shoots of grass poke up everywhere, and the blackberry bushes are unfurling again from all the old, dead brown. Old Oak is waiting. She smells the best after a rain, her bark soft and damp with a sweetness there. I start to sit down, to look out at the camp, when suddenly the fur bristles at the base of Bingo's neck—a silent signal that I need to be careful. As I turn, Deer is flying above the rotten fence, clearing the blackberries on the other side like a creature from an old myth. When she lands though, something is terrible and wrong. Her left side is soaked with blood, a darkening, fist-sized hole by her shoulder. She falls to the ground and shudders, softly bellowing the sounds of sorrow. Her big, brown eyes dart around and ask how this happened and why.

Bingo doesn't bark or try to go closer. He sits still, like he knows this is sacred—as if Deer could be me or could be him, could be Mom or Toby or any of us. I know to stay away, too, to let her have her wildness—to say goodbye and leave this place in her own way. The tears are warm on my face as I sit where I am but tell her over and over again with my mind, *I'm sorry. I'm so sorry, I'm sorry.* I hope she remembers all the beauty she got to feel in her strong, young body before this awful moment when her eyes stop darting and there's no more steam rising from her nostrils and she is still.

—

I sit down at my tree and the salt tears keep falling. My stomach fills up with air—I'm a balloon again and might finally float all the way up now, into outer space and gone forever. It's hard to swallow. My stomach is all hot knives making me bleed but I don't want to look down there. I am hot and cold at the same time, sweating and shivering. Bingo licks my face and looks worried, nudges my arm because I'm lying on the ground now and not moving except for my body's shaking. The dirt smells rich. The dampness from the rain cools the heat in my chest, cools this fire ripping through the middle of me.

The head I created for myself on the ground is gone. My acorn eyes and leaf ears have been eaten or washed away. I am headless again, flat and empty.

Maybe Mom will come home soon and figure out where to find me. Maybe she and Gary broke up tonight, and she will feel sad but not for very long this time. She will take me to the clinic, and the doctor will remove the gnashing teeth with a special tool, and make the knives and the blood stop with medicine. The doctor won't take me away from Mom, she'll just give me what is needed to make everything better. Mom and I will watch the next matinee and walk by the river again to find the Great Blue Heron. Mom will say she changed her mind and that I can be called Rocky if that's what I still want.

Or maybe people from the camp will wander up, wanting to meet this beautiful tree up close, and then find me curled beneath it. They will know what to do because they care for each other in the camp. Bingo will show them the way to our house, and it will be okay then. Mom will have come back from the store with milk because I drink so much of it now. She will even warm it up like she did when I was younger, and the knives will be soothed to sleep from all that creamy whiteness. Or maybe my dad will come back, my real dad, all the way from where he's been, and recognize me. He'll feel an animal pull, an instinct to appear, even after all this time has passed and all these things have happened. He'll come just in time. He'll find my journal and know who I am, like no time has passed at all.

When I was little, I remembered things from before. Once I asked Mom how to hold on to that earlier time when everything about being here made sense. She looked at me like I was an alien visiting from a UFO, the weirdest person she'd ever met. I wanted her to tell me how to not forget everything I learned the last time.

I watched her and wanted her to have a real answer but she didn't know what I was trying to say and now I don't know either.

My insides are turning slack and I understand that I am leaving this place—going back to where all the babies live before they come here. Mr. Kohl taught our class about infections and mine grows stronger and stronger, its own kind of wild animal. Here it is inside me, upending roots, starting a stampede, gnashing. I can just let it live now, maybe it is the wildest part of me, has been all along.

I concentrate as the fading picks up speed—I'm getting lighter—I have never been this light. I focus my mind on telling Bingo and Moonshadow that I will make a home for them in the other place, the place after this one—for them to take the time they need here, but to come when they're ready. I tell them there will be lots of little brothers to play with there. When they don't want to be here anymore, all they have to do is lie down long enough and it will be over—all this churning will stop—and they will be on the other side, in the forest where I'll be waiting.

The sky is a mottled gray with dark and light patches and flecks of white are falling now, framing the long branches of Old Oak, texturing the sky—a vast blanket covering all of us—a late, unexpected snow. The green buds came too soon, but there's a chance they'll still make it. This blanket of snow covers Mom, Moonshadow, Bingo, the owls, Old Oak, and the people in the camp who are singing an old melody that drifts over this wide, snowy field, alive.

This blanket covers Toby in the hospital and Cherry holding his hand. It covers Foxy in her crop top and sneakers and her wounds. It covers Great-Aunt Josephine in the east as she pays attention to all the numbers and all the signs—translating their complicated meanings. It covers Gary and Claudio and Edwin and White Richard too—and all the other ones who can't stop hurting and fighting and lashing and molesting and beating and yelling and raping and punching. Maybe they're the ones who need this blanket the most; it's the only thing that could let them rest—into the small children they were before all the scary things happened.

If they could just close their eyes into stillness and let themselves be held by the air and the land and the animals, they would see how being alive can sometimes feel like a miracle, even as you let it go.

Deer wakes up as if from a nap, stands on all fours, shakes the pine needles off her wooly back, and takes a bite of a new bud starting to open on a low branch as the snow melts. And I am standing, too, next to her. We are not cold or hungry or hurting. We are about to go to Blue Frog Lake and then past there—to the denser forest, to the river, to the mountains, and then even beyond all that.

Deer says it's hard to explain and it's a very long walk, but every step will be something new. I lean my head against her flank, and she is warm and smells of rich musk, smells of bone and muscle and pumping blood, of life. My body, too, is all these things, and there is brown, shimmering fur coming in. I scrape my two front feet across the ground, and listen to the sound of hooves.

ACKNOWLEDGMENTS

Thank you to everyone at Torrey House Press. I love what you're striving for here in the West. Thanks to the Willamette River (where I'm from) and the Elk River (where I'm going). Thank you Karen Nelson, Pam Houston, and all the amazing teachers I've learned from through Writing by Writers. I really appreciate you.

Thank you, Mom and Grandma. I'm so glad you raised me to pay attention to the animals and the plants and the clouds. Thanks to all my friends, teachers, students, and creatures. Thank you, Susan, for all those walks and talks along Big River. Thank you, Hillary, for our incessant laughter that sometimes makes no sense and which cannot be stopped. Thank you, Jade and Lewis, for the long-term epistolary love. Thank you, Kien, for the wresting match several lifetimes ago. Thank you, Holls, for the humor and the depth. Thank you, Heather, for the words and the music and the silence—for all of it, especially the soft. Thank you, Mark Ali. I know you're listening to really good jazz somewhere out there. I miss you.

Thank you, Western Hemlock. Thank you, Licorice Fern. Thank you, Salal.

ABOUT THE AUTHOR

Charlie J. Stephens is a queer, non-binary, mixed-race writer from the Pacific Northwest. Born and raised in Salem, Oregon, Charlie has lived all over the US working as a bike messenger, wilderness guide, high school English teacher, and seasonal shark diver (for educational purposes only). Always encouraged by their grandma and mom to write stories, putting pen to paper has long been a part of their life. Currently living in Port Orford on the southern Oregon coast, they are the owner of Sea Wolf Books & Community Writing Center. Charlie's short fiction has appeared in *Electric Literature, Best Small Fictions 2020, New World Writing, Original Plumbing* and elsewhere.

TORREY HOUSE PRESS

Torrey House Press publishes books at the intersection of the literary arts and environmental advocacy. THP authors explore the diversity of human experiences and relationships with place. THP books create conversations about issues that concern the American West, landscape, literature, and the future of our ever-changing planet, inspiring action toward a more just world.

We believe that lively, contemporary literature is at the cutting edge of social change. We seek to inform, expand, and reshape the dialogue on environmental justice and stewardship for the natural world by elevating literary excellence from diverse voices.

Visit www.torreyhouse.org for reading group discussion guides, author interviews, and more.

As a 501(c)(3) nonprofit publisher, our work is made possible by generous donations from readers like you.

Join the Torrey House Press family and give today at www.torreyhouse.org/give.

Torrey House Press is supported by Back of Beyond Books, the King's English Bookshop, Maria's Bookshop, the Jeffrey S. & Helen H. Cardon Foundation, the Sam & Diane Stewart Family Foundation, Diana Allison, Karin Anderson, Klaus Bielefeldt, Joe Breddan, Carl Buck, Laurie Hilyer, Frederick Klass, Susan Markley, Kitty Swenson, Shelby Tisdale, Kirtly Parker Jones, Katie Pearce, Molly Swonger, Robert Aagard & Camille Bailey Aagard, Kif Augustine Adams & Stirling Adams, Andrea Avan-taggio & Peter Schertz, Patti Baynham & Owen Baynham, Rose Chilcoat & Mark Franklin, Jerome Cooney & Laura Storjohann, Linc Cornell & Lois Cornell, Susan Cushman & Charlie Quimby, Kathleen Metcalf & Peter Metcalf, Donaree Neville & Douglas Neville, Betsy Gaines Quammen & David Quammen, the Utah Division of Arts & Museums, Utah Humanities, the National Endowment for the Humanities, the National Endowment for the Arts, the Salt Lake City Arts Council, the Utah Governor's Office of Economic Development, and Salt Lake County Zoo, Arts & Parks. Our thanks to individual donors, members, and the Torrey House Press board of directors for their valued support.

Printed in the USA
CPSIA information can be obtained
at www.ICGtesting.com
LVHW051139030424
776227LV00003B/12

9 781948 814980